I0586828

FOREVER YOURS

IN THE DARK, BOOK TWO

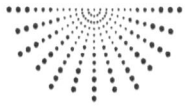

VIOLET HAZE

STOKED PUBLISHING HOUSE

Forever His ©2015, 2019 by Violet Haze

Cover Design from Designs by Dana
Stoked Publishing House
ISBN-13: 978-0-9992261-6-2

ATTENTION

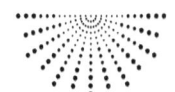

1

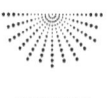

OWEN

THE WOMAN BEHIND THE COUNTER, with her wavy shoulder-length dark blonde hair and bright red lips, doesn't belong here.

Her curious eyes dart around the room even as she makes the customer's drinks as if she's searching for something — or someone, perhaps.

Since this is the first time I've laid eyes on her, and I'm here each evening even if other things occupy my time during the day, she must be none other than the new hire.

The odd thing is, even though I'm fairly sure we've never been introduced, she seems familiar. And there's no doubt in my mind, that if we knew each other intimately, I never would've forgotten such an occurrence.

"I would ask what you're staring at," Joy remarks with a soft laugh as she slides into the seat across from me, "but something tells me it's the beauty behind the counter who has caught your attention."

Reluctantly dragging my gaze away from the object of my intense scrutiny, I look at my loyal assistant with an indulgent smirk. "I assume the final decision on hiring her took some convincing on your part to the manager."

"A little, but he seemed as impressed as I was. She came with wonderful references and incredible skills. Plus, she's easy on the eyes and has sold more drinks tonight than we've sold all week. Worth every cent she asked for, and more, but we won't tell her that."

"Is she?" Flicking my eyes toward the woman for a brief second more, I return my attention back to Joy along with a single brow raised. "What's her name?"

"Rachel Dawson, or so she says."

Taking a sip of my drink before setting it down on the table with a decisive tap, I chuckle and give my watch a quick glance. "You don't believe that's her name?"

"A girl that beautiful wanting a job here with her background? I'm instantly suspicious, as you've instructed me to be, sir."

"She does strike me as someone I've met before. There's no way I would forget fucking her, however, making it likely I've run into her elsewhere."

Joy doesn't even blink at my blunt statement since she's often involved in setting up my intimate sessions with women and used to frank talk. "I doubt it, as she told me she arrived here not even a week ago, and she's taken the rooms above the bar as part of her compensation."

Interesting. "Ah. Now, in that case, I'm genuinely intrigued and must introduce myself to my newest employee."

"I would be careful if I were you. She looks like the biting type."

Chuckling, I pick up my glass and savor the last of my drink before rising to my feet while winking at her. "My favorite kind of pet, as you're aware, so that'll hardly put me off, Joy."

"Don't scare her away," she admonishes me with a long and overly dramatic sigh. "She's the best hire we've had in ages."

Because I'm the owner of this establishment — and also due to the fact I've never gotten involved with an employee despite my joking about pets — I don't bother responding to her impassioned plea, striding toward the bar with focused determination.

The woman pauses in her duties as I approach, the cloth in her hand stopping on the surface of the bar as she watches me, unflinching with a curiosity equaling my own as she stares back with her light golden-brown gaze.

Stopping in front of her, I hold my hand out for her over the counter and smile at her waiting for me to speak first, and am more than willing to break the ice. "Owen Chandler."

I introduce myself this way as she should recognize my name, if not my face, as it's something Joy would've told her during the interview or upon being hired. Since she's not from around here, she wouldn't be generally aware of who owns this place, nor what I do for fun on the side.

And as she puts her hand in mine and shakes it firmly, she confirms my assumption with a single nod. "Rachel Dawson, sir. Pleased to meet you."

"My pleasure, I assure you, along with welcoming you to the team. I hope you thoroughly enjoy working here."

"I'm sure I will," she replies with a bright smile, her rigid stance softening as she lowers her shoulders and slips her hand from mine before dropping it to her side. "The pay alone is worth the men licking their lips and the women staring at me with daggers in their eyes."

A quick glance to my left and then right to prove her comment on point makes me grin wider as I focus back on her with a small inclination of my head, even as I avoid commenting on her appearance to keep things professional. "I'm pleased the pay meets with your approval."

"Wouldn't have taken the job otherwise."

I might've believed her statement had there not been a soft and almost small hitch of her breath before she spoke the words. It makes me wonder why she might lie about not taking the job, but not enough to ask.

"Well, Miss Dawson, if you need assistance or have any concerns at any time, please let either Joy or I know and we'll be happy to help however we can."

"Thanks. I will."

Before I can respond, a customer catches her attention for a drink by raising his empty glass in the air, and she tosses me a quick smile before walking toward him without another word.

Not even three seconds pass before Joy is standing beside me and places a firm hand on my arm to gain my attention, which I give her with only a small bit of reluctance as her interruption prevents me from checking Rachel out further. "Owen, we should get going. You've got the wedding tomorrow and need your rest."

"When did you begin acting like my mother, Joy?"

My question is without heat, as it always is. Joy's eyes soften with emotion and her lips curve up in a gentle smile when my hand covers hers with a light squeeze. She doesn't respond as we head toward the door because we both know the answer to the question.

Four weeks after my mother's death, leaving

behind a devastated husband and sixteen-year-old son, is when twenty-one-year-old Joy moved in. Her mother had worked at the university with my father and told her daughter everything. So, after a brief conversation with my dad, Joy decided to become helper-slash-chaperone to both of us for a little while.

Yet, she never left after becoming my best friend, closest confidante, and business partner, cementing her place as a permanent part of the family with her devotion. And with my father's death two years ago, just a few months after my thirty-second birthday, Joy's the only family — albeit chosen — I have left.

And that's why she takes good care of me, as I do her because that's what families do for one another.

It's what I keep in mind as we get into the car, reminding myself that taking care of Joy means I have to behave when it comes to business. Because of that, I absolutely mustn't become intimately acquainted with the bartender, even if she's among one of the most beautiful women I've ever seen.

"NOTHING LIKE WATCHING A WOMAN YOU would've loved having as your own marry another man."

After muttering the words, I put an obnoxious fake pout on my lips and pair it with a glare as Joy laughs softly.

"You never had a chance with her, Owen, and you damn well know it," she says after quickly smothering her reaction with the palm of her hand at my scowl and rolls her eyes from where she sits to my right.

There's nothing to do except smile in response and straighten in my seat because even if I'm aware of that, I'm sure as hell not going to admit it to anyone. "Shh. I'm trying to watch a wedding here and your babbling's ruining it."

"Hush, then."

Chuckling, I turn my gaze back to the bride, and the woman I will only ever dream of having as mine. Simone is as beautiful as ever in her wedding gown, and for a split second, I curse my stupidity at approaching Isaac that day to help get the two of them to work out their differences and reunite.

Then, I shake my head at my foolishness. Ridiculous to think that way even for a moment, because these two genuinely love each other, and are now the parents of two boys after the birth of their second son, Elijah, four months prior. Although Isaac had desired marriage almost immediately upon Simone's return to living with him, she made it clear she wanted to wait until after the baby was born, and today's ceremony shows she got her way.

No surprise there since I would've done anything to make her happy as well, especially after everything she's gone through. She deserves a man who treats her as if she's a queen, and much as I adore her, she's happy even if it isn't with me.

As much as I shouldn't admit it, though, watching them pledge their lives and love to one another causes an old and familiar ache to build in my chest. Other than my voracious sexual appetite keeping my bed warm with women who share in my particular interests, none of my relationships have been long-term, let alone leading toward marriage and a family.

It's my own damn fault, and perhaps a bit of nature's too since it's rare to meet a woman who makes me feel as if we would make a good match beyond the bedroom. Except with Simone, nobody has come close in a long time, and some of that is due to me becoming more selective as the years go by.

I know what I'm looking for, I just need to fucking find it.

Looking around at the guests isn't necessary to know I won't find the woman I'm looking for through my friends, since the gathering's rather small, with only Simone and Isaac's closest non-single friends and staff attending their intimate wedding. And yes, Isaac and I have a friendship of sorts even with everything that went down, but only because Simone insisted she felt nothing for me beyond friendship.

Great for her and her relationship, not so much for me; however, I'm happy to have any place in her life because she's a beautiful person inside and out.

When they kiss after being declared husband and wife, Joy sighs with pleasure beside me, and I find it necessary to smother a groan at the way those two wrap their arms around each other to kiss with abundant enthusiasm.

Then, in a sudden whirl of activity, we're being ushered out of our chairs as the setup of the room is redesigned by the staff, and it doesn't take long for the reception to start. Joy wanders off to get something to eat from where the food is put out a few minutes later while I take a seat at one of the tables closest to where Simone and Isaac sit near the front of the room.

Helen speaks to Simone for a moment before heading to a door off to the side, and just as Joy returns to the table with a plate full of food, Helen re-enters the room cradling Elijah in her arms while Malik toddles along beside her. He takes off at the sight of his mother, flying into her arms as she gets out of her seat to crouch low to the floor, only to stand up and hold him above her head while he giggles.

"Go say hi already," Joy mutters, lifting a brow

at me when I glance over at her, and nods in Simone's direction as she takes a bite of food without saying another word.

She doesn't need to, as the moment I start to rise Simone's voice calls out to me, and I look up to find her walking toward me with Malik on her hip. Moving to meet her halfway, she doesn't even pause when she gets close, choosing to slip her arm around my waist and hug me from the side while Malik babbles incoherently from his perch.

Putting an arm around Simone's upper back, I give her a return squeeze filled with all the warmth and affection I have for her, and after a moment, she steps away with a grin up at me. "I'm sorry I didn't get a chance to greet you before the ceremony, but I'm so glad you made it."

"I told you I would be here, even if there were a blizzard, which thankfully there wasn't." We both look at the tall windows — which line both walls and let in a ton of natural light — to see the bright sun reflecting off the snow already on the ground. "Looks like the storm they predicted decided to hold off another day."

"Yeah. I'm quite happy about that too."

"If you weren't happy today, I might be the only one in the room who didn't question your sanity." Leaning down close to her ear, I give into the urge to tease her a little in my usual fashion, chuckling as I whisper, "You married the wrong man, after all."

"Shh," she responds with a laugh, reaching up to slap me gently on the arm, and looks back over her shoulder to smile at Isaac before returning her gaze to mine. "You two might get along now, but he'll kick your ass if he hears you talking to me like that."

Straightening, I shake my head and take a step back even as I say, "Not a chance in hell. At best the fight would end in a tie."

She laughs again and rolls her eyes, which light up as the beginning notes of the first dance begin to play, and with another glance at Isaac rising from his seat she holds Malik out to me. "Mind keeping an eye on him for a dance or two?"

"I'd rather be dancing with you," is my answer even as I take Malik from her, his little hands coming up to grab onto my shirt as Isaac reaches us and holds out his hand for Simone to place hers in.

With a look back at me, she takes his hand and says, "Thanks!"

They're whirling around the room a minute later, Simone's happy laughter filling the air, and for a brief second, Malik is as quiet as me while both of us watch his mother dance.

Then, he bursts into tears, Joy rescuing him from my cluelessness when he won't calm down no matter what I do after a couple minutes. With a final glance at the dance floor, I stride off to the bar for a drink or two in an attempt to drown my feelings until the things I know I shouldn't want are the last thing on my mind.

2

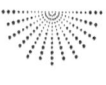

RAMONA

THE MAN IS as handsome as I expected he would be.

In fact, he looks so much like his father, a man my own father showed me pictures of when I asked about him as he had no photos of the son I've been promised to marry since birth — Odin Vasnetsov.

In this country, he's known as Owen Chandler, and I know I can't blame him for the fact his parents fled with him when he had been a mere child of eight himself, as my father helped them disappear for their own safety.

However, the promises his father made to mine — and my dad being a man of his word no matter how inconvenient he found the vow after this long — meant my whole life has been on hold because of this agreement.

At my age, I should've married a man ages ago, and already have a house filled with children as well. Instead, against my father's desire to keep me close to home, I planned a trip to find the man I'm promised to marry.

He wasn't the only one unhappy with my decision.

My childhood friend, Maksim, begged me to run off and elope after declaring himself in love with me. His declaration hadn't really surprised me as I suspected he's had feelings for me for a while, but I still told him that a promise made should never be broken without the consent of the other party.

Plus, as much as I love Maksim and he would make an excellent husband and father, I've never thought of him as more than a friend. I didn't know, however, if it was because of being promised to someone else had prevented me from ever actually dating or exploring my connection with others, or if he just didn't spark any romantic desire in me.

Now that I'm here, I know it's the latter, and want nothing more than to be honest about who I am and what I've come for.

However, I don't want Odin to find out that information before I'm able to get a good idea of the sort of man he is, so I became Rachel Dawson, an identity which cost my father a good amount of money from the same man he hired before. As Rachel, I'm a simple woman from a dull background just looking to start a new life away from her overbearing parents.

It's not far off the mark with the way my father has sheltered me my whole life, but since someone tried to kill his best friend along with his wife and son, I suppose I've never been able to blame my father for the way he acts.

With my perfect English skills and no sign of my accent — something which took a lot of practice to accomplish — there's no way for anyone to think I'm from anywhere else except the States. And no way to connect Rachel Dawson with Ramona Dorokhova, the little girl five years his junior and declared his future wife to bring our families together forever.

Nobody knew their identity except for my father, and with the help of a P.I., getting information about his life here had happened within weeks of my request. Locating him had been easy, and after a few phone calls, my experience in bartending was established after I saw his restaurant hiring one. At no point had I considered what I might do if I didn't get hired, but I'm glad things worked out that way.

Especially tonight when he walks in wearing a tux, appearing deliciously disheveled and more than a little bit lost.

I keep thinking of him as Odin in my head. I'm so afraid it will slip out uninvited that when he spoke to me for the first time yesterday, the marked pause before my response had been intentional. I had to make sure I didn't call him the wrong name, because no matter how hard I try, he's been Odin to me for so long I'm not sure I'll ever think of him as Owen.

Not even my father calling him by his American name — something he only did in private in case I ever met the man — had managed to accomplish that in all these years, since we'd been introduced briefly when I was three right before he and his family vanished. His name has stuck in my heart despite efforts to call him otherwise.

So I mostly refer to him as, well, 'he' or 'him' in my thoughts because it's neutral and I'm hoping this keeps me from saying the wrong thing. Perhaps more time spent in his presence and around others referring to him as his known name will assist me as well, but it's hard to say.

His eyes skim the room, landing on mine right as I place a drink in front of a customer who thanks me by slapping the money on the counter before walking away, and my stomach flips as a delighted grin lights up his whole face.

I respond with a smile of my own even as I wonder why he's looking at me like that. He met me yesterday and barely knows me, yet he strides toward me with such purpose I'm unable to do much except watch in fascination.

Perhaps he feels the same pull I do, the one

which has intensified since setting eyes on him in person, and keeps growing the more I think about this gorgeous man putting his hands on every inch of my body.

My thoughts about this are interrupted as he gets closer to the bar, a strong whiff of whiskey greeting my nose as he sits down making it obvious he's been drinking quite a bit already. He's not wobbling or incapable of walking, but I think if he orders more than a drink or two I will have to cut him off. Even if he is my boss, it's still my job to make sure my customers aren't too wasted.

When he takes a seat, he chooses one right in front of where I'm standing behind the bar and plops down with a heavy sigh. But the grin remains on his face as he says, "Hello there."

His words aren't slurred, which surprises me, and I keep a reciprocating smile on my face while addressing him. "Long night?"

"You've no idea, I assure you." Bringing his hands up to the counter, he taps it briefly before folding them together in front of him and ordering a drink.

Without responding, it's only once I've given the drink to him and he takes a sip that I notice the woman who hired me hadn't come in with him. It's probably inappropriate for me to ask, but since Joy told me she's his assistant, my internal questioning finds its way out of my mouth. "Nobody with you tonight?"

"Nope." The look on his face as he pauses, staring at me as if he wonders why I would ask such a thing, and lifts his brows when my eyes flick to his drink. "Ah. Joy wanted to stay longer at the wedding, so I left her the car and hailed a cab."

That's a relief. He'll take a cab home, which means there's no need for me to cut him off unless he gets rowdy, and he doesn't seem the type to start a fight even with his size. Although I'm sure he'd happily finish a brawl with little issue. "Wedding?"

He takes another drink and then shakes his head. "Don't want to talk about it."

"Sure."

My attention is diverted by another customer as Jay, the bartender who will take over once I leave for the night, arrives. Seems as if every time I turn around following that, Jay's pouring him another glass, and I clock out when done with everything as my shift ends.

After a moment in the back talking with the manager, I walk back out and stop abruptly at the sight of a woman in a tight black skirt and a shiny tank top with her arms wrapped around his neck.

Screw it. I'm just gonna call him O.

And not only does O look not interested by the bored expression on his face, but he's visibly drunk at this point. So, without even thinking about the potential consequences of overstepping any boundaries, I stomp over to where he sits and tap on the woman's shoulder from behind.

Her arms slip from around his neck as she whirls around with a scowl, her eyes widening as she lifts her head to look me in the eyes since I'm about six inches taller than her. I only know this because she's about the same height my mother reaches when she stands next to me, and my mom is five-foot-five.

I take after my father, and in moments like this, it comes in handy because many women I meet are intimidated by my height.

She almost proves me right when she takes a step to the side, but after a glance at O — who merely flicks his gaze between the both of us with a smile before taking another drink — she squares her shoulders and deepens her frown. "What's your problem?"

"I don't have one, but he doesn't appear to want you hanging on him."

She laughs, tossing her red hair over her shoulder along with a glance at O as he throws back the rest of his drink, and brings her focus back to me with a shrug. "Who are you, his girlfriend? Because your thoughts on the matter don't mean shit otherwise. We were getting along just fine."

"No, I'm not his—"

She doesn't even let me finish before cutting in with a sneer. "Duh, I know he doesn't have a girlfriend, so fuck off because what we do is none of your fucking business." Stepping close to him, she slips her arm around his, her hand slipping down to clasp his tightly while leaning down to speak close to his ear. "Come on baby, I'll take good care of you at my place."

His eyes find mine after she says that, as if he's waiting for me to object again, and when I don't he nods at the woman before standing up. That's when he wobbles, his hand coming up to slap the counter, and the woman laughs.

Laughs, as if it's the funniest thing she's ever seen, and I wonder how many other times she's gotten him to go to her place when he's like this. Either way, not a chance of that happening with me here, and I step forward while signaling Jay to assist me.

"He's not going anywhere with you. He's too drunk to consent to anything at this point, and will be going home alone."

"Fuck you," she says, her hand clasping his tighter and tugging on it, huffing when he doesn't move. "I've taken care of him many times. This isn't any of your fucking business, bitch, so get out of our way."

"You need to let go of him," Jay tells her as he walks out from behind the counter and stands next to me, crossing his arms over his chest as he gives the woman a nasty look. "Consent doesn't only apply to women, and if he's too drunk to walk, he's too drunk to fuck someone who takes him home. You need to leave, now."

"He's fine," she hisses, giving O an expectant look, but when he only stares back at her with a blank look, she yanks her hand away and flips me off. "Fine. Screw both of you, I'll talk to him tomorrow and get both of you fired."

She storms off before either of us can reply while Jay steps forward to steady O, who lifts a hand to rub at his forehead while still not speaking.

Jay, with an expectant and confused look, asks me, "Now what?"

"Well, you have to work, and I don't know anything about where he lives or if Joy would even still be awake this late." Thinking about what to do, I finally blow out a breath and shrug while pointing upward. "Help him to my place upstairs. Can put him in my bed and if I can't get ahold of Joy, I'll take the couch."

"Are you sure?"

"Yes. I mean, he's smashed and can barely stand. Besides, I can take care of myself, and he'll probably be out the moment he hits the bed." Taking my keys out of my pocket, I hold them out to him. "Go ahead. I'll take care of the bar while you do that, and go up when you come back down."

It's obvious he's skeptical, but after a moment, he takes the keys and walks off with O stumbling along beside him. And ten minutes later, when I enter my apartment and go to check on him, he's out cold while lying diagonal and snoring softly.

I manage to locate Joy's number, but she doesn't answer, so I just shut the bedroom door and head into the living room. Exhausted from my long day, it's not long before I pass out on the couch while thinking this is not the way I thought having O in my bed would happen for the first time, if ever.

3

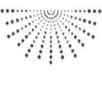

OWEN

I KNOW before I've even opened my eyes that I'm not in my own bed.

My head is pounding, and even though I don't want to force my eyelids to lift, the fact I know it's not my home makes figuring out where I'm at imperative.

Another fact is that I had too much to drink last night. I rarely drink so much I can't recall what happened the evening before, but since I'm in a strange bed and can't recall whose bed this is in an instant, this qualifies as one of those times.

Glancing around the room after my eyes have adjusted to the daylight, my initial conclusion is this isn't the room I usually wake up in when Sally manages to get me to go home with her, so thank fuck for that. She always has perfect timing, coming upon me when I've had a bad day and don't stop drinking when I should because it's what she enjoys doing and I'm usually happy to fulfill her needs.

There aren't many women I engage with on a regular basis, but Sally's an exception since we get on so well. Yet doesn't seem as if she did that last night, which is good since I probably wouldn't have turned her down, even if she wasn't set to receive services until next week.

But if not Sally's place, then whose bed is this? This room doesn't provide many clues being as sparsely furnished as it is: a bed, a nightstand with only a lamp on it, the closet closed, and a dresser with a mirror on the back. Nothing else, not even personal items.

Sitting up nice and slow, I spot my suit jacket hanging over the back of the chair, and with a quick glance down realize I remain fully clothed. Fucking incredible. Not only was I drunk, but I passed out on whoever brought me home with them.

With a sigh, I stand up and grab my jacket, shaking it out before tossing it over my shoulder. Then, after shoving a hand through my hair, I walk over and open up the door, the smell of pancakes greeting me. Striding out, my surroundings are taken in on auto-pilot, leaving me clueless at the lack of pictures on the hallway wall.

Ignorant of where I am is how I remain while stepping into the empty living room, and at the sound of a woman softly humming, I head toward what must be the kitchen.

And as I push the door in, two sudden realizations halt me in my steps. One, I finally recognize that I'm in the apartment above my restaurant, and two, that means the woman standing at the stove in a long shirt with her legs bared must be none other than my new bartender.

"What the fuck?"

She lets out a squeal of surprise at the sound of my voice, spinning around as one hand flies up to cover her heart, and stares at me with round eyes. If I weren't extremely fucking confused on how I ended up in her bed, I would find her reaction amusing and her attire arousing. Instead, I place my jacket on the back of the chair by the table, and cross my arms over my chest as I ask, "Want to tell me how the hell I ended up in your apartment, Miss Dawson?"

Recovering from her brief shock, she turns back around to face the stove and flips the pancake over, her response filled with amusement. "If you aren't aware of that one little detail, then it's good you didn't go home with that vulture."

"Vulture?"

"Red hair, beady eyes, ugly attitude. Threatened to get me fired when she saw you again. Ring a bell?"

Chuckling, I pull out a chair at the table and

sit down. "You prevented Sally from taking me home with her?"

"If that's the woman I'm talking about, then yes. Jay assisted, especially with getting you up here to bed." She pauses to flip the pancakes again, then lifts the pan and slides them onto the plate next to her on the counter. "She was rather angry when we told her you were too wasted to consent and, therefore, she had to leave you alone."

Keeping a straight face is impossible at the thought of Sally's reaction to being told that, and my laughter has Miss Dawson tossing me a smile over her shoulder while turning off the burner and then picking up the plate.

She walks around the room after placing the pancakes in the center of the table, grabbing two empty plates and forks as well as two glasses. It would've been polite to offer assistance, but my attention's diverted by her legs, and by the time it comes to mind she's already sitting down across from me with orange juice in hand.

After pouring herself a glass, she holds the jug out to me and smiles without saying anything as I take it from her. From there, total silence falls between us while we eat, and right as we finish is when I notice how quiet it is.

Too quiet, with none of the usual busy sounds of traffic or people yelling outside, and a sharp glance toward the window above the sink makes the reason why crystal clear — the snowstorm has arrived in the form of a complete white out.

"Yeah, nobody's going anywhere today." Dragging my gaze from the window at her words, she's staring at me and shrugs when I meet her eyes with raised brows. "They've shut down the city. I called Joy this morning to let her know you were here with me since I couldn't get ahold of her last night."

"Did you? I'm surprised she isn't blowing up my phone at me being alone with you and unable to leave."

She doesn't even blink at this, bringing her glass to her lips and drinking the rest of her juice before replying. "I told her you were sleeping and would call after you woke up."

Smirking, I glance down at my plate, over at her, and then at the window before shaking my head and focusing back on her. "This is strange, isn't it?"

"A little, yes, since you can't leave. But don't expect me to entertain you," she says while standing with her plate and glass in hand, nodding toward the living room. "If you want to watch TV, I have cable. I'll take this unexpected day off to do extra cleaning, along with my usual laundry day."

No pretense from her, I like that. She doesn't give a shit that I'm her boss, no doubt treating me as if I'm anyone else who is staying longer than originally intended.

"Sure," I agree while standing up, grabbing up my plate and walking toward the sink. "Do you know how much we've received so far?"

"No, I must've missed them saying the amount."

"Guess so." Placing my plate and fork in the sink, I pivot on my heel only to see her walking away without another word into the other room — apparently she's not into small talk.

Slipping a hand into my suit pocket, I lean back against the counter and pull out my phone, discovering a text from Joy. "*Please tell me you didn't sleep with her.*"

I know she's joking around since I've never overstepped professional boundaries, but it doesn't prevent me from teasing her back due to the current circumstances. "*Not yet but I might. I'm stuck here in her apartment thanks to the weather. Wondering if I'm serious or not is what you get for staying behind last night.*"

Not even three seconds pass before her name pops up on the screen, and I can't keep the laughter out of my voice as I hit accept and put the phone to my ear. "Yes?"

"You're unable to leave? I thought Miss Dawson was joking."

"She wasn't. No need to worry yourself, however. Miss Dawson has made it clear I'm to entertain myself and stay out of her way."

Joy sniffles as if I've offended her with the

suggestion, although we both know I haven't. "I'm not bothered. I was glad to hear you were all right, though. Waking up to a missed call from Miss Dawson had me on alert since I knew that's where you were headed last night."

"Yes, well, be thankful she and Jay prevented Sally from digging her claws into me again. I may need to get a restraining order at this rate."

I'm not serious, yet Joy responds like there's no humor in my tone at all, as always. "You could always stop drinking to the point you blackout, Owen."

"I rarely have that much to drink."

"Not little enough if this keeps happening."

She truly does act like my mother sometimes. "I'm aware and not bothered. We're both aware Sally might be crazy, but she's harmless. Just has a fetish—"

She interrupts me with a scoff of protest. "Yes, I'm well acquainted with Sally's preferences, thank you. I have no need for you to repeat them for me."

Laughing, I turn to face the window and find the thickness of the snow coming down amazing. "You know I wouldn't torture you that way, Joy. But do you think I should inform Miss Dawson about the agreement Sally and I have in place? I would say I can't believe she tried on a night that wasn't hers, but I'm not."

"Perhaps a better idea is to find somewhere

else to have Sally approach you from this day forward. No need to spread around what you do with your private time among the employees." She pauses, then lets out a breathless sounding giggle. "I will admit them telling her you couldn't consent is amusing. At least we know both will help prevent those sorts of incidents from happening on their watch."

"Right." Pausing at the sound of Miss Dawson humming, I look at the doorway in the exact moment she walks past it. Her legs are still uncovered and I wonder if she realizes she's not wearing any pants, or if she's merely oblivious to the effect such a state might have on a man. "I suppose you have the whole day off now, Joy. Any plans?"

"No. I needed to go shopping since Christmas is next week, but I suppose I'll simply have to order online now and pay for two-day shipping so everything will be here in time."

"Have a good time. We'll speak again later."

"Yep."

She hangs up without waiting for a reply, leaving me to wonder what I should do now. I don't watch television much, but I have nothing else with me to do, not even my laptop. So, walking into the living room to sit on the couch, I grab the remote off the coffee table and push the power button.

The selection is as terrible as I figured it might

be, but I turn on something that sounds funny after reading the description, and pull out my phone to browse while halfway listening to the station I've chosen.

She comes and goes from the room, at one point carrying a laundry basket into the kitchen, where the washer and dryer are hidden behind another door if I recall correctly. I've had this place a long time, and the only person who has been up here since renovations is Joy, but I remember most of the layout now.

When she walks back into the living room, she stops in the doorway, locks her eyes on mine, and puts her hands on her hips. "You can stop looking at my legs any minute now."

I don't even bother explaining myself, just grin at her before flicking my unapologetic gaze down to her legs, and back up when she starts tapping her foot. "I would apologize, but I find it impossible to ignore the fact you're walking around not wearing pants with a man sitting here. And I'm a leg man."

She rolls her eyes, although her face flushes a little as she glances away. "I told you, it's laundry day. If I had clean pants to put on, I would just so you'd stop staring."

"I like them."

"I believe your inability to stop ogling them is proof enough of that, but it's not appropriate, is it?"

Shrugging, I lift my hands facing up and smirk at her, knowing I'm being unprofessional and enjoying the blush on her face too much to stop. "Nobody around to say whether it is or isn't. We'll keep this conversation between us."

She opens her mouth, only to snap it shut and step closer, her eyes squinting as she stares at my chest. With a wiggle of her finger up and down at her own chest, she lifts her gaze to mine and asks, "What is that? A tattoo?"

Her eyes widen in wonder, which is the usual reaction of someone who sees I have tattoos for the first time, and it's amusing. Brings to mind the way Simone had reacted upon seeing me in the room that day, scanning me from head to toe with curiosity and more than a little bit of fear due to the circumstances.

But Miss Dawson has no reason to fear me, of course. She's got no idea about my business on the side, and as long as she works for me, it's not something she'll find out either. While finding a new place to meet with Sally is annoying, Joy is right; there's no reason anyone at work needs to know about my fulfilling of sexual fantasies.

"Yes," I say to her, unbuttoning the top of my shirt a little more as she's straightens, and point at the base of my neck where the tattoos start while teasing her. "From here down, deliberate so they don't show when I'm suited up. I can show you them all if you'd like, but it would involve me getting undressed."

"Ah, no thanks." Clearing her throat, she takes a step back, moving to clasp her hands in front of her before declaring, "You know, I think I forgot to put detergent in the washer, I'll be right back."

My laughter follows her out of the room as she practically runs from it, and tells me everything I need to know about whether Miss Dawson is attracted to me or not.

Even if teasing her would prove an enjoyment, I do need to remain professional, and I promise myself I will once we're no longer in such close proximity. A glance out the window makes it evident that won't be today, however, and with a wicked smile, I wait for her to return while pondering all the ways I can keep that radiant heat on her face until I can leave.

4

RAMONA

Right as I'm finishing up the dinner dishes and turning off the water, the lights flicker for a few moments, and then die.

"Shit," I mutter beneath my breath, standing still while hoping they come back on, and whirl around as light flashes toward me.

O stands there with something in his hand, using the light on it to find me before he moves it toward the floor, and heads my way.

"I sure hope the lights come back on soon," I tell him as he stops in front of me, the light on his phone bright enough I can see a little of the room and of him as he looks past me toward the window.

The storm has let up a little, but there's at least two feet of snow on the ground, and at this rate, will be three feet by morning.

"Me too," he says while moving his focus back

to me with a grimace as he shuts off the light. "It's gonna get fucking cold in here tonight if not."

He can't see the alarm on my face at his words, but chances are in this storm, the lights won't come back on at all tonight. And that means we're alone together, in the dark, with nothing to do except keep each other company.

Not that I'm worried he will do anything. Other than teasing me, which seems to be a big part of his personality, he hasn't done anything since discovering he's stuck here to make me think he will be inappropriate. I started the conversation earlier about his tattoos, and for him to say they went all the way down…was he serious? I'm pretty sure he was, so that's why I told him I had to check the washer because I almost wanted to accept his invitation to show me.

If anyone was thinking inappropriate things, it was me, because I do find him physically attractive. I hope he didn't notice, but something tells me he probably did with the way my face kept giving away my emotions so clearly. My father always told me it was the one thing he loved about me, because when it came to how I felt about something, he could always tell if I were being honest or not.

That's the last thing I need with O right now, hands down. Second is this unexpected time allowing me to be near him, but it will give me the opportunity I need to get to know him, I suppose. And at least I've got leggings on now.

Of course, thinking about him staying here thanks to this storm, I'm wondering how the hell we'll survive the night in the freezing cold with my lack of blankets. I don't have many things since I haven't been here long, and my apartment doesn't have much beyond the essentials because I don't plan on making this my permanent home.

Why hadn't I considered this might happen? I should have considering the amount of snow we get back in northern Russia, but I suppose I never thought he would be in my place with me and require covering as well. Stupid of me, but not much I can do now.

This isn't how I saw my day going. I thought I would wake up, he would go home, and I would go to work. Instead, he's been here, and I've had to keep myself busy so he doesn't ask too many questions I don't want to answer. Lying to him is something I wish to avoid altogether, so the less I say, the better, until I'm ready to tell him the truth.

"Miss Dawson, are you all right?"

His voice jars me out of my thoughts, the warmth of his hand seeping through my shirt as he puts his hand on my shoulder simultaneously, and the unexpected touch has me blurting out one of my biggest fears. "Not really, I don't like the dark."

"Ah. Well, at least you aren't alone. I think that

would be worse at a time such as this." I feel his hand slide down my shoulder as if he's trying to comfort me, then down my arm until it finds mine, and clasps it tightly with his. "Let's go sit in the living room. It'll be more comfortable than standing here."

"Okay."

I'm usually not so agreeable, but I honestly don't like the dark, and yes it's nice to not be alone during this. Not that I will tell him that out loud. I remain silent as he turns the light back on and leads the way, making sure I'm sitting down before he takes the seat beside me.

"If you feel like you're going to panic," he says in a soft tone, "just lean into me. Sometimes just having someone close can ease the way darkness makes you feel."

Probably shouldn't get that close, but talking will keep me calm, so keeping a conversation going with him seems like a good idea. "Have experience?"

"Actually, yeah. I was scared of the dark as a boy, but my mother would come in and sit next to me so I wasn't alone. But when that wouldn't work, she would climb into bed and tuck me into her side."

"You don't seem like you're the type who's scared of anything."

"We all have fears. Some are just better at hiding them than others." He laughs, his arm coming around my shoulder in a light, friendly way, and the feel of his breath on my ear is what tells me how close he is to me. "I don't fear the dark anymore, though."

Even though every part of me is screaming to pull away, to tell him being this close shouldn't be happening, I don't move an inch because the weight of his arm comforts me. Plus, I'm curious and want to gain his trust so he'll tell me everything I need to know quickly. "What do you fear, then? Anything?"

"Fire."

He says the word softly, almost devoid of emotion, but I know all about why he's afraid of fire. His family home going up in flames, he and his parents barely escaping with their lives because they were sleeping when it started. A fire determined to have been started intentionally.

Aware before I even ask the question that he may not want to answer, or even be able to, I ask it anyway. "Want to talk about why?"

"Nope." He remains close to my ear, his left hand coming up to rest on the fabric just above my knee, and the arm around my shoulder inches my body a little closer to his. "If I make you feel uncomfortable at any point, just tell me. I merely wish to distract you from anything which might induce anxiety. Is it working?"

"Yes."

And it is. His touch, innocent as it is, does

things to my insides I've never felt. How would I have? I'm not a virgin, but I don't have much experience with men. In my late teens and early twenties, I rebelled from the idea I was promised to someone else, dating even against my father's wishes because it was easy to do on campus. But those few times were with boys my age, guys who still fumbled around and thought of nobody except themselves, which I allowed because I hadn't known better. They got off and I was left lying there wondering why it didn't feel all that great.

I only lasted two years on campus before my father put an end to my rebellion by saying I must live at home unless I wanted to be cut off. Not that the threat was necessary — nobody says no to my father. He had too much power to make my life miserable. As he once told me, caring didn't mean letting me have my way; it meant he must take care of me and make sure I'm on the right path, even if I disagree.

Sure, I could've said no, but I was young and had nothing to land on my feet with. And it wasn't like he limited me, or kept me at home and didn't let me go out. It meant I went to school, and I got a job as a server, and he kept me so busy I had no time to date men who wanted nothing more than someone to have sex with and nothing else.

When I asked my father why it was so important I marry this man's son, instead of me finding someone else, he told me it was a matter of honor and loyalty, and if one doesn't keep their word, then they have nothing else someone may rely upon them for.

He explained that if I didn't follow through on his promise, it looked bad for the whole family, not just on me. And Ivan Dorokhov wasn't okay with appearing anything less than perfect to anyone, not even for his family.

I think in this country, if I told someone that, they would say I should do whatever I want because my happiness is what matters. But my father is important to me, and I love him, which is why I came here to find Odin. If a promise is broken, it will be done with honor, and with making sure the other half of the promise isn't waiting for it as well.

And sitting here, with O close physically and yet so far otherwise, I have no idea what will happen. It's too soon to tell, but the fact he won't discuss why he's afraid of fire tells me he probably remembers his life in Russia, and makes me wonder if anyone knows who he really is beside me — like Joy.

"Miss Dawson?"

Startled at his raised voice, I clear my throat. "What?"

"I asked you a question."

"Oh." Dammit, I feel the heat creeping up my face, because I was so lost in my thoughts I hadn't hear him speaking to me. "I'm sorry, got lost in thought. What did you ask?"

"Must have been some serious thoughts." When I remain silent, he chuckles and removes his hand from my knee, pulling away a little as he says, "I asked if you were cold. The temperature is dropping quickly in here, so perhaps it's best to get some blankets."

"A little but, I've only got the comforter on my bed. I...I haven't really gotten everything I need or might need yet."

"Trust me, I noticed when I woke up this morning how little belongings you have." He removes his arm from around my shoulder and, after clasping my hand in his again, stands up while pulling me with him. "I suppose we'll have to share the bed then to make sure we both stay warm."

The thought of having him laying to me, in my bed *with* me, when a mere touch can tangle my insides and feelings without much effort, makes me wish the lights would magically return and the snow would stop. I could say I'll sleep on the couch, but he's right. It's cold out, it's going to get colder in here, and with one damn comforter to share, we'll have to be in the same bed cuddled up to one another.

Damning the world for ruining my plans, I don't even waste my breath protesting, letting out a soft sigh while giving in to the inevitable. "All right."

He turns the light on his phone on and leads the way once more, leaving me following in his wake and hoping this isn't going to turn into a pattern.

I FEEL HIS AROUSAL AGAINST MY BACKSIDE AS HE snuggles close behind me, and it's impossible to ignore. He hasn't said anything since we got into bed an hour ago, but I wonder if men find it a problem that they can't hide their attraction for a woman when they are this physically close to her. At least, not like a woman can, since it's less outwardly...prominent.

We've been forced into close intimacy to share warmth because of a storm I should've known was coming. And desiring each other is a problem, something we have to ignore because we can't act on it.

Not can't in truth, but definitely shouldn't. Because as far as he knows, I'm Rachel, and I'm his employee. It's a boundary he nor I should cross, and frankly one I absolutely shouldn't without him knowing who I really am. It would be dishonest.

And yes, I'm already deceiving him, but not with evil intentions. I met him just over forty-eight hours ago, with today being the only time we've spent together at all, and it's not enough to know his real character.

However, I will admit I want to know more about him, especially his life here all these years. He's obviously done well for himself, and while I'm here to decide whether or not he's a man I'd like to marry, I have to consider the fact he has a life in this country. He may not want to go back to Russia; he may want nothing to do with his home country, or me, at all.

His hand sliding around front to rest on my stomach makes me inhale sharply, his touch foreign and warm even through the light sweater I'm wearing, pleasing me in a way I hadn't thought it might. Who knew such a simple touch would make me wish for him to do more in an instant?

I hear him breathing slow and even, so believe he moved his hand in his sleep, even as his hand presses against my stomach to move our bodies closer. Not possible since I'm fairly sure there's no space between us to spare.

Neither of us had removed any of our garments, but mixed with this comforter and his body heat, I'm actually getting a bit too warm. It's making it hard for me to fall asleep, and just when I'm considering getting out of the bed, he grumbles into my neck, "Fuck, I think I need to take off some of my clothes."

Sighing with relief, I pull away from him and slip out of the bed, lifting the sweater of my head before saying, "I was just thinking the same damn thing. You're like a damn heater."

I can't see him moving around, but I hear him, and he laughs at the same time the bed creaks, letting me know he either got out or back into it. "It's handy when there's just nudity to contend with."

"I'll take your word for it."

After a short moment of silence which seems normal and not awkward like it should've been following his statement, he clears his throat at the same time I hear him pat the bed. "Come back in, I'm all done."

"Me too." With my tank and leggings still on, I climb back on the bed, turning to my left side like before as I lay down. "Hopefully, now we can sleep."

He moves back into position, his arm coming around my front again, and resting where the bottom of my tank goes just over the top of my pants. He leaves his hand there as the rest of his body lines up with mine, and the feel of his muscular form against my back gives me a hint as to what he hides beneath those suits of his.

I feel small against him, which is a feat all of it's own, considering his height of about six-three only puts him roughly four inches taller than me. But I know that's only one factor of it; the other is build, which when it comes to him, is broad-shouldered but not bulky. I've no doubt he could crush me in his hold, and part of me can't wait for the show of strength I know he's more than capable of exhibiting.

Then, right as I figure he's not going to respond and shut my eyes, the soft brush of his lips against my shoulder makes them fly open as quick as they closed. My whole body stiffens in his arms as I gasp, the sensation evoked by his kiss shooting down to where his hand rests, and pulling my reaction in all different directions.

He doesn't let go, though, his hand playing with my shirt even as he groans and says in a low voice, "Sorry. It was an impulse I've been trying to ignore since we met. I'm not sure I can behave any longer being this close to you — unless my attention is unwelcome, of course."

Appreciating his honesty, and intuitively understanding the internal war I'm sure he's fighting with me being his employee, rationality tells me I shouldn't give in. But this gorgeous man I've come all this way for wants me, which makes me want to feed the banked passion between us, to just go for it and hope for the best outcome.

What's the worst that can happen really? He'll find out everything and not want to marry me, leaving me free to find someone who will. That's it.

Right. Nothing is that simple, but for the

moment, the lie I tell myself is enough. Giving into what I want, what he wants, is as easy as turning in his arms and sliding my arms around his neck.

So that's exactly what I do, leaving no doubt about what my answer to his question is.

5

RAMONA

ONCE MY ARMS lock around his neck, O doesn't waste any time in taking what he wants.

He rolls me onto my back and captures my mouth with his own, his growl of approval lost between us as his tongue forces its way inside with little more than a small press of demand trailed across my lips.

Although his body is completely flush with mine, the fact he leans a bit to the left tells me he's using his left arm to keep his weight off me, while slipping his right hand underneath my tank. The heat of his hand warms my skin as it travels north, and pure pleasure bursts through me when he cups my breast in his palm, causing me to gasp in shock when he pinches the nipple hard enough I'm not sure if it hurts or feels good.

He moves to the other side before I can decide and repeats the motion, placing my decision firmly in the feeling good category as my whole body lifts toward his in a plea for more. He chuckles into my mouth, pulling my tongue into his mouth to suck on it before releasing me and pulling away.

My head spins at the pace, arms dropping from around his neck as he straddles my body. Both of his hands move my shirt up my torso and over my head, the sound of my shirt landing on the floor the only indication he's tossed it aside.

I gasp as his hands move to the waistband of my leggings, and his whole body goes still as he asks softly, "Problem?"

"No." Both excited and nervous, I swallow hard and take a deep breath while relaxing my whole body, even as I admit, "I'm…I'm not that experienced in this, is all."

If possible, his stance grows more rigid at my admission, although the tenderness mixed with the trace of humor when he speaks tells me I simply caught him off-guard. "You're not a virgin are you, Miss Dawson?"

Wincing at him calling me that, I shake my head before realizing he can't see either motion in the pitch black of the room, and let out a heavy sigh. "No, I'm not. Just not much experience. And please, call me Ivy."

"Ivy?"

"My middle name. I prefer it."

It's not a lie, technically. My father's name is Ivan, which makes my middle name Ivanovna, and telling him it's Ivy is as close to the truth as I'll come right now. I'd rather tell him this than have him call me by that completely fake name. But I shove it aside, because dwelling on this whole thing is ruining the mood, and I've no intention of changing my mind.

"Ivy," he repeats again, although this time I can tell he's testing it out, rolling it around his tongue and trying to decide if he likes it; if it fits me. "All right, Ivy it is. And you must call me Owen."

"I could, but I think I prefer to simply call you O."

"There's nothing simple about an O." He punctuates the statement by pulling my leggings and silk panties down my legs, tugging them off and tossing them to the side before I realize what he's implied, and making me glad the darkness hides my whole body flushed from his teasing. "However, you can call me whatever you like, as long as you're screaming it by the end."

I'm tempted to ask him why I would be screaming. I mean, I know sex should be more enjoyable than it's ever been when I've done it, but to the point of having that sort of reaction? He distracts me from inquiring, however, by moving his body over mine again, pinning me to the bed and invading my mouth once more as if it belongs to him.

This time, I put my hands on his shoulders, finding them bare and smooth to the touch, and wish there was enough light his tattoos were visible. Of course, the fact there isn't any light or heat is how we've ended up this way after all.

He diverts my attention from that train of thought by reaching down with his right hand and lifting my left leg until it's hooked around his hips, moving to do the same with the other leg before bringing his focused touch back to my breasts.

At the same time, I simply want to let him do his thing and experience every sensation by focusing on it, a quick rub back and forth of my foot where it rests tells me he's stark naked…which means he took off all his clothing when we were trying to get comfortable earlier.

I feel his hardness between my legs, our bodies lined up nearly perfect for joining, and when I lift my hips, he rocks back into me, accompanying the stimulating movement with a pinch to one of my already taut and sensitive nipples.

When he takes his mouth off mine, lifting his weight off me a little as he starts to travel down my form, I grab his hair in an unexplainable panic and whisper, "Where are you going?"

"Nowhere." He laughs and continues downward, even as my hands grip his hair, and answers my question by placing a soft kiss on my lower abdomen. "Plant your feet on the bed and spread your legs a little."

Feeling as if my whole body is aflame and flushed, I do as he says, my hands covered by his before being gently pulled away from his hair and placed flat down on my stomach just above where his head is.

He licks the spot where he kissed me a second ago before gently blowing on it, eliciting a gasp from me along with a tremble as I attempt to keep myself in the position desired. And when he chuckles again, his breath brushes the spot between my legs where I ache for his touch the most.

"Hold yourself open for me," he says in a firm command as one of his hands slips under my ass and gives the cheek a squeeze. "My hands will be otherwise occupied."

I'm glad for the darkness since I've never touched myself in front of anyone, sliding my hands down to fulfill his request while taking comfort in the fact he can't see me. Not sure I'm ready for that, which is foolish really, considering I'm about to have sex with him.

The first touch of his tongue against my clit surprises me even though I should've expected it, the sensation both arousing and strange in its intensity, and I wish my hands were free so I could anchor myself before the feeling carried me away.

He circles a few times with his tongue, slipping one finger inside me and curling it upward before sucking on my clit gently. He caresses the sensitive spot inside me, making me see stars behind my eyes when I close them, and the dual attention in that area is enough to get my body climbing rapidly toward orgasm.

Another finger joins his first as he alternates between licking and sucking, and when the pressure and pleasure build to the point I know the orgasm is going to take over, I move my hands to the bed and grip the top sheet tightly in my fists.

That's when he removes his hands and mouth completely, leaving me teetering on the edge of what no doubt would've been the best orgasm I've ever had, even by my own hand.

With a dark chuckle, he says, "I didn't say you could let go, so now you'll have to wait a little longer."

"What—?"

He cuts off my question by getting off the bed, grabbing my ankle and pulling me to the edge, making me shriek from the abruptness of it. Flipping me over before I catch my breath, he smacks my ass — the sudden sting making me cry out again — and says, "Don't move."

"O—"

"Shh. I'll take care of you," he reassures from somewhere to the left of me, making me wonder what he's doing for a second until he's back and grabbing my hips with a squeeze. "On your knees."

If I weren't dying for the release he's denied me, his bossiness would irritate me, especially since he doesn't even ask me nicely. But I get up on my knees even while telling myself that's something we'll have to discuss later, and wait for him to give us what we both want, the chilly air adding a bit of an urgency to the moment.

At the sound of foil tearing, I realize why he walked away before, leaving me feeling foolish for not thinking of such a tiny yet significant detail.

He teases me with his arousal, moving it up and down but not slipping inside, and when I move back in encouragement, he pulls away with a dark snicker and asks, "Do you want it fast or slow, Ivy?"

"I don't care." Lowering my body so my head lays on the bed, my hard and pert nipples brushing the sheets, and I grip the sheet with one hand to keep myself steady while slipping the other down between my legs. "But if you don't get me off quick, I will happily do it on my own."

My warning works as he slams deep into me with one hard thrust, his hand grabbing my arm and moving it out of the way while saying harshly, "Don't you dare touch yourself again without my permission."

No man's ever told me not to touch myself before, and instead of being repulsed by this show of dominance, it unexpectedly excites me because it's obvious he's keeping a tight rein on his urges. Perhaps my admitted lack of experience is preventing him from doing things he normally likes, but I don't want him to hold back. I want him in all his glory because I want to know what I'm getting into with eyes open, and something tells me this interlude is barely breaching the surface.

"O." Breathy, my whisper is a demand and a plea as I bring my hand back up near my head and anchor myself entirely in case he lets go like I know he wants to, wiggling my ass to tease him even more while pushing his buttons. "As long as you keep me waiting, I'll do what I want. What the hell are you waiting for, both of us to freeze?"

"Fuck." He hisses the word, his fingers digging into the flesh of my hips as he pulls almost all the way out before thrusting back in hard enough to make us both moan. "Next time, a gag is in order so that smart mouth of yours can't talk back, but until then…"

There's no more speaking anyway as he effectively silences me by fucking me so fast the only noises coming from my mouth are involuntary ones of enjoyment. One hand leaves its position on my hip and slips between my leg, rubbing me in perfect timing to his thrusts, and right as my whole body starts to shake from the imminent orgasm, his touch is gone and he stops moving inside me.

Left hanging again, the fucker, my body instantly retreats from the edge. "No!"

"Ivy," he coaxes with another hard thrust before pausing, his hand going back to my clit and teasing me by circling around it yet not touching me directly. "If you want permission to come, you'll need to beg me for it."

Pinned in his hold, he moves slow and gentle, the movements meant to keep me just short of the edge without allowing me to tip over, and it's pissing me off. I know he would if I told him to and get myself off, but nothing will come close to being the mind-blowing orgasm waiting for me if I were to simply give in to his demand.

A tiny shift on his part, a stroke mixed with a touch swiftly brings me back to the brink and leaves me teetering at the peak while my whole body shakes, and I give in because there's nothing I want more at this moment.

"Please," I beg him, relaxing every part of me while I practically sob the words. "Please."

"Please what? Ask nicely like a good girl would."

"O…please. Let me come. Please?"

And he does, pinching my clit between two fingers while fucking me hard and fast once more, my orgasm exploding on the second thrust, so strong I learn how one would make a person scream from the force of it.

"Ah fuck," he groans a second later with a final thrust, his hold on my hips almost punishing in his grip as he comes too, only to let go as he slips out and steps back. "Let me clean up, I'll be right back."

I don't know how long he's gone because one second I'm waiting for him to return, and the next I'm opening my eyes to the light of the morning only to quickly discover he's already gone.

And it's not long before I regret letting it happen at all, wondering if it's going to cost me my job and the chance to get to know him.

TWO DAYS HAVE PASSED AND I HAVEN'T HEARD A word from him.

Yesterday had originally been my day off, and when I didn't receive a call changing that or asking me to come in, I ended up hiding in my apartment all day trying to reassure myself we had both given into our attraction in a weak moment.

Worse, it's all I can think about as I head into work tonight, and made worse when he walks in with Joy on his arm, even though his eyes burn into me from the moment he enters.

He sits down where he can watch me, and for a few glances, I look at him right when he looks at Joy until finally our gazes meet across the room. His sudden wink confuses me, and I bite my lip wondering what it could possibly mean since he doesn't even get up to come this way, until I realize he's not going to and shake my head at how disappointed it makes me feel.

So turning to assist another customer who

catches my attention with a snap of their fingers, I shove aside any thought of O and what he makes me feel to focus on my work for the rest of the night.

By the time I finally catch a breath toward the end of my shift, he's nowhere to be found, and after clocking out, I head upstairs now feeling as if having sex with him had been a major misstep. And naturally, one I need to find a way to fix fast.

What I didn't plan on was arriving at the top of the steps and seeing someone from home standing outside my apartment door waiting for me.

Maksim's smile of greeting disappears at the sight of my sudden scowl, and stalking toward him, I stick my key in the door while hissing, "What the hell are you doing here?"

I don't wait for an answer while opening the door and heading inside, where he follows me and shuts it behind him before speaking in Russian. "I miss you, *malyshka*. This is silly, both your father and I agree, and you should come home now."

Tossing my keys on the table, I point an angry finger in his direction, wondering why the hell my father would tell him where to find me. "I'm not your baby, so don't call me that. I told you I don't think of you that way."

"Ramona," he says, switching tactics but not fooling me as he takes a step closer with his arms out, and pulls me into his embrace with a sigh.

"I'm sorry. I need you with me. You are always on my mind, and I worry about you here, this far from home."

I don't return his hug, pushing him away after a second, and shaking my head while turning away. "I told you I'm not the woman for you, Maksim. You need to return home and find another woman to take as your wife. I'm here to get to know Odin, and you're going to ruin it."

Half expecting him to get upset like he did when I turned him down back home, he shrugs instead and turns toward the door even as he says, "You are making the wrong choice. And you will soon discover your mistake when you realize the man you're seeking will never give you what you want. But don't worry, I will be waiting for you at home, *myshka*."

He leaves, slamming the door behind him hard enough to make me wince, and the first thought on my mind is to call my father to see if he told Maksim where I was. And if he had, why he would do such a thing? I know he's my friend, but giving up O's location seems a reckless thing to do regardless.

Only I never get that far because the doorbell rings five minutes later, and half expecting Maksim to return for another stunt, I yank the door open to discover an angry looking O outside.

"I thought you looked familiar, *Ramona*," he hisses in Russian, taking a threatening step forward while the color drains from my face as it occurs to me that he must've come up while I was arguing with Maksim. "It's good to know you take after your mother."

Fighting him fruitlessly as he grabs me, his hand comes up to cover my mouth and nose, and it's not long before I pass out while wondering just what the hell O's going to do now that he knows who I am.

6

OWEN

"I KNOW you slept with her, " Joy says with a roll of her eyes as we take a seat in the booth at the restaurant two days after the storm. "The expression on your face when you look at her gives you away."

We're sitting so the bar is straight ahead of our table, affording me the perfect view of the gorgeous woman standing behind it.

Ivy, of course. Strange she wants me to call her that, but I think it fits her, so I will happily do as she wishes...for now. "Wasn't trying to hide it. The moment I couldn't leave her place without endangering my safety, I knew fucking her was inevitable."

"No, you didn't. You've never crossed that line before."

Sometimes I wish she didn't know me from the inside out, which is all my fault, and nothing can be done about it now. "Yes, I know. Even told myself that, but at that moment, impossible to resist. And I've behaved myself, remaining completely professional just now by not going over to greet her."

"Have you talked to her outside of work since then?"

"No. This is the first I've seen her since leaving the other morning, even though I left my number for her to call."

"A woman who doesn't fall at your feet, I think I like her a bit more than I already did."

"You would because you like anyone who might put me in my place as well as you do when I deserve it."

She nods, pointing at me with a smirk. "Key words there are 'deserve it' and you do this time."

"Perhaps, but what's done is done." Leaning toward her, I speak fast to prevent Joy from responding since the waitress is approaching the table. "Having enjoyed the time we spent together, I plan to further our acquaintance, and since this is the first time I've felt this way for a while, I'll ask you not to ruin it for me."

Laughing as if that's the funniest thing she's ever heard me say, she manages to nod her understanding right as the waitress stops at our table with a bright smile directed toward me. After taking our drink order, she walks away, and my focus goes back to the bar where I find Ivy staring at me.

She doesn't look away this time as she's been doing since we walked in until I wink at her and she bites her lip before shaking her head and turning away.

Dammit.

Looks like I'll have to scrap plan A — wait for her to talk to me on her own — and go for plan B — show up at her apartment once she's off for the night and gone upstairs.

It's a long wait, with the restaurant busier than it's been for a while, and after we're done eating, I leave with Joy to finish business before taking the night off to focus on pleasure.

～

UNBELIEVABLE.

This night hadn't turned out like I thought it would at all. Instead of telling a woman I was interested in dating her, I find out she's come all the way here to track me down, and she's the enemy.

Not Rachel Dawson. Not a beautiful, fascinating woman who calls herself Ivy.

No, instead she's Ramona fucking Dorokhova, daughter of my father's best friend and betrayer, the man who had tried to kill my entire family.

Of all the woman in the world to break my rules for and end up not only fucking, but feeling something for…shit, I'm an idiot.

Joy seems as dumbfounded as I am because she knows the whole sordid tale from my childhood, and when I called her from the stairwell to tell her to be in the car and ready to leave, she had no idea that I would bring Ramona with me.

Shit, another rule of mine broken when I chose not to walk away. No, in all actuality, I broke the fucking law because I took her against her will in my feelings of betrayal and anger.

Not only that but now she's a prisoner in my home, naked and locked inside a windowless, empty room in a secluded part of the house with nothing in it except the bed she now rests upon.

The only way to enter is through my chamber, and when she awakens, she'll discover all of that along with the shock cuffs locked around her neck, wrists, and ankles. Handy contraptions made just for me by a whiz friend of mine, and meant to deter undesired behavior more than hurt or cause pain, and they work wonderfully.

If I believed in hell, I would definitely be going there for daring to tread upon her rights as a human being this way, but I'm too angry to do the honorable thing. If this makes me an asshole, so be it, because I'm downright confused at this whole situation.

She got a completely new, false identity to come here and worm her way into my life. Why? Sure, the storm wasn't her fault, but everything else? The way she listened to me talk about my mother and my fear of fire…and the whole time she knew exactly who I was.

Again the question is why, and I won't even consider letting her go until she answers it. The problem is, now I know her as the consummate liar she is and it may be hard to figure out what the truth is, or to even get it from her, as she may not know what honesty entails.

The desire to get answers right away is the reason I'm sitting in her darkened room on the floor, waiting for her to wake up now for over an hour, and jump to my feet at the sudden sound of her coughing.

When she speaks, it's in our native language, the sound of her voice raw and filled with emotion, the cuffs clinking in the dark as if she's tapping them together. "Oh my god, where the hell am I?"

Conscious of the fact there's no way for her to know she's not alone, I remain silent and motionless, waiting to see what else she will say while believing herself the only one in the room.

She doesn't disappoint, the sound of her crying evident in her sniffles as she says random things to herself out loud, the cuffs occasionally making noise when they rub together. "What am I going to do? I have to figure out where I am. It's so dark in here. God, where has he taken me? I deserve this, but I wish he would let me explain.

Something is wrong, lying about who I am shouldn't have made him that angry. If only he would've given me even a second to say why I've come here, but he didn't. I've never had anyone look at me with so much hatred…"

Unable to take any more of her babbling — and what sounds like bullshit to me as well — I deliberately cough soft and slow, letting her know I've been here the whole time as her voice trails off.

Her intake of breath is sharp and loud in the dark and otherwise soundless room, her words trembling with fear. "Odin? Is that you?"

The sound of my birth name on her lips, the name I haven't heard in the eighteen years since my mother died, sends my already intense anger shooting through the roof.

"Don't fucking call me that," I spit out, storming over to the bed and slapping my hand down on it with no idea of whether I'm close to her or not. "You don't have permission to say my name, do you understand?"

"No." She stumbles in her reply, the mattress moving beneath my hand telling me I was close to her, and now she's moved away in the fear I wanted to make her feel. "I don't. I'm so confused. My father—"

"I don't wish to hear about your father. I don't even want to hear about you. I want you to quit talking, right now, and simply listen to what I say."

"Please, Od—"

Pissed off at her inability to realize the seriousness of her situation, and my seconds ago warning to refrain from speaking my fucking name, I press one of the five buttons in the center of the remote. Her reactionary howls of total surprise as the ankle cuffs give off a short and useful two-beat warning zap make me smirk.

"That's what will happen every time you ignore what I tell you to say or do. The only time you speak is when I ask you a direct question." The only response is the sound of her increased sniffling with an occasional hiccup of a sob, and after a pause to make sure she's not going to stupidly open her mouth, I get on with it in a deliberately bored tone. "What you didn't know about me is that on the side, I fulfill fantasies. Some are simple fetishes, which I won't disclose for privacy reasons, but others are...more in tune with what you're experiencing right now. Women want the fantasy of being a sex slave — so they're kept in a soft bed, with collar and cuffs, and treated with care as long as they service me as I desire."

She sobs harder, and for a moment, I wonder if I'm going too far, because despite what I'm implying there will be no sexual activities between us. At least, there won't be if either of us are unwilling, and I don't know about her, but at this point in time, I don't want to fucking touch her at all. I want answers, and then depending on what she tells me, she may gain her freedom if she's truly innocent.

However, knowing her father, I'm skeptical of her having no culpability in whatever the hell's going on here.

"You are to keep your gaze on the floor unless I specifically tell you to look at me. When I ask you a question, you will respond in the shortest way possible at an average speaking level, calling me 'sir' at the end of your reply, and at no point are you to say anything with what might be considered a bratty or nasty attitude. Do you understand?"

She doesn't respond immediately, and after counting to three I tap the button so her arms are zapped this time, and through her wails she yells, "Yes, sir!"

"Excellent. Now, if you don't mind, I'm exhausted and heading to get some rest. You can't leave this room from inside it without the fingerprint-only pad on the wall, so attempting to escape will be a fruitless exercise for you. Not to mention there's no lights on in here if I don't turn them on, and no windows, so it might take you a while to get around. Good things there's nothing for you to trip on since the only furniture in here consists of the bed you're on."

She whimpers, making me glad she can't see the smile on my face because I'm always impressed at my fucking ingenuity when it came to modifying this room for my private purposes. "If you're a good girl and follow all my directions, you'll earn more than just time spent doing nothing, perhaps even books to read and paper to write on for entertainment. But if you displease me, or lie to me, you'll spend a lot of time alone in the dark with nothing to do except think about how to improve your attitude."

Walking toward the door, I press my fingers into the pad, and when the door unlocks, I look back and tell her one more thing while pushing it open. "Oh, and when Joy brings you your meals, do not speak to her or ask questions. She has nothing to do with you being here, but will report everything you say and won't help you no matter how much begging is done. Sleep well."

And because I'm not a total dick, a single press of the button on the side of the remote turns on a singular indestructible light panel at the bottom of the wall across from her bed, giving the room a little light so as to prevent her from having an anxiety attack.

Then I exit the room, making sure the panel snaps shut behind me, and head to bed wondering what secrets tomorrow will bring regarding my new, treacherous pet.

ADDICTION

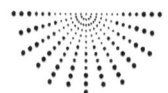

RAMONA

Day two of being locked in this room and O hasn't returned since the first night.

However, Joy arrives with breakfast minutes after I wake up, as she has since the morning after my arrival, and places the plastic tray on the floor a few feet from the bed.

She doesn't speak as she goes to stand by the door, where she'll remain until I've eaten everything on the plate. As if I would starve myself — I might be confused and more than a little angry at this whole situation, but I'm not stupid.

Slipping out of bed, I walk over and grab the platter before returning to sit on the edge, picking up the plastic fork and taking a bite of the scrambled eggs.

Another thing that's been the same with breakfast. It's always delivered by Joy on a paper plate with a plastic fork with eggs, toast, and bacon, along with a side of orange juice.

It's delicious, and after I'm done, Joy takes the tray and leaves the room. Yet, unlike yesterday, she returns shortly after and stands at the door with it open.

"You need a shower. Follow me, please."

The fact she speaks catches me by surprise, and before thinking, I respond while standing. "Joy—"

"I would advise against talking and simply do as you're told, Miss Dorokhova," she interrupts in a flat and distant voice, turning away without even casting a glance at me. "Keep your hands clasped in front of you while walking, and come this way as I've said."

Although O warned me, it's hard to believe Joy would treat me this way, but I suppose my deception pissed off both of them considering how loyal and dedicated she is to him. I can appreciate that kind of loyalty though as it's how I feel about my family, especially my father, and it's crystal clear that O and Joy consider themselves a family unit.

Placing my hands in front, I lace my fingers together and walk toward Joy, who waves me through the door before following me and shutting the panel behind her. Instantly, the fact we're in another room instead of a hallway stops me in my tracks, and astonishment takes over at the sight before my eyes.

Dark wood paneling covers three walls — one with a bay window — while the fourth has floor-to-ceiling bookshelves filled with books. In the center of the room is a four-poster bed which appears to match the color of the paneling, and the plush carpet beneath my feet seems to be ivory.

The comparison to the room I'm in with all its white, from the bed to the walls, is stark. And although I haven't cried since arriving, sadness creeps in at not knowing what's going to happen, and being left to wonder is the worst. I prefer O come into the room and scream at me, yell at me, tell me what he thinks compared to what he's doing now.

Ignoring me, mixed with the endless silence all day long, is unbearable. But not even with that is this worth freaking out over because I don't think causing trouble will get him to free me any sooner and, as long as he isn't hurting me, I can put up with this little bit of humiliation he's providing.

"This way." Joy grabs my elbow and leads me across the room toward the window before turning right, and stops in front of a pad on the wall.

Placing her fingers on it, she steps back as a panel clicks open to reveal the large bathroom hidden behind it, and I'm truly fucking fascinated by all the high-tech shit in this house which clearly cements the fact O is quite well off.

"Go on," she says while releasing my elbow. "You've got ten minutes to shower. Everything you need is already in there, and there is a timer. You can see it inside on the door as well, so don't ignore it. The light will go off when time runs out."

After stepping inside, I whirl around and hold up my arms to display the silver cuffs wrapped around my wrists. "What about these?"

"It's fine to shower with them. They're waterproof." She steps back, pushes a button, and as the panel starts to close she says one final thing. "The timer will begin in five seconds. Don't dawdle."

She wasn't kidding. The light comes on the second the lock clicks, a digital clock on the door buzzing while starting the countdown, and with a curse, I walk over to the shower and turn the water on.

The fact O's kept me completely naked is probably the only positive to the ten-minute limit. I've never taken one that quick, but I suppose there's always a first time for everything.

Finding everything I need — although is it really necessary to only give me a one-bladed razor? — I have two minutes to go when I'm done with the shower. Getting out, I rub myself down quickly, comb my hair, and then turn to the sink to brush my teeth with the items supplied.

I have to say, I'll appreciate brushing my teeth at a sink more in the future since yesterday Joy had merely supplied a cup with some water and a toothbrush with some paste on it in the room while making me do it in front of her.

Unable to decide if there's a point to this system they use, or if they are showing me things can be given or taken away at any time. Probably the latter, but I won't know for sure since I'm not allowed to ask.

And sure, I could talk and ask Joy questions, but what would be the point? I didn't enjoy the zapping the first night, and I would prefer to avoid having it done again, so I've decided to just say nothing.

The moment the light goes out, the door opens and Joy pops her head in. "All right, time's up."

She steps back as I walk out, glancing down at my hands — which I've clasped together as she instructed me to earlier — and nods while shutting the door. Then, she leads the way back to the bedroom and leaves me all alone once more.

Unsure what's going to happen next, I study the room as I've been doing since arriving. Right before Joy visits in the morning, the ceiling lights come on, and at night when they turn off, the panel on the wall turns on — not much, but enough to keep the room out of total darkness.

That's how I know O's not a monster. Angry about something, yes. Did something he shouldn't, absolutely. But the fact he cares enough not to leave me in the literal dark thanks to being aware of my fear tells me a lot about his overall character.

Now if I could just understand why he's mad and clear up why I lied, things will get better. I mean, I hope that's all it will take. Maybe it will even happen today — he'll come back and let me explain and then it'll be all over.

If not, I may start talking to myself again to keep myself awake. Sleeping as much as I have isn't good for me, but there's nothing else to do; not like there's a TV in here to watch or something.

Wait. That gives me a thought, and I scan the room thinking maybe he's watching me. I mean, if I had a house with a room like this that is obviously meant to keep someone captive, cameras would definitely be a good idea.

And even though a simple inspection of the room with my eyes doesn't find any obvious cameras, a wicked thought that comes to mind has me climbing into bed and laying on my back. I may not have a lot of sexual experience with men, but all those nights I've spent alone and aroused with no relief in sight led to self-exploration that will allow me to give O quite the show if he's watching.

Covering a breast with one hand, I skim my fingertips of the other one down the center of my torso until reaching my stomach, where I flatten my hand out.

Bending my knees, I place my feet level on the bed while spreading my legs, and move my hand down between them to cup myself. Closing my eyes while caressing and kneading the breast cupped in my hand, I let my mind wander to the other night with O and the way he made me feel.

Slipping two fingers inside myself, I imagine they're his, stroking me just like he did, and wishing his mouth were available for a repeat performance. But he nor his mouth are, so with a disappointed sigh, I curl them up to stroke my g-spot with a slow back and forth motion, and use the pad of my thumb to stimulate my clit.

I hear his voice in my head, telling me I'm not allowed to come without asking first and am a little ashamed to admit I want to hear him say it again. I should be so angry at him right now that I don't want him to ever touch me, but instead, I'm highly aroused and desiring his caresses more than any rational woman would in this situation.

Just thinking of his words has them springing to mind, and I swear his voice is loud and clear in my head, telling me to hold myself open to his mouth. Then, the voice tells me if I want to come,

I need to beg him for it. And because I want O to see this but not know how much he's inspiring my actions, I silently mouth the words begging for his permission to come instead.

My body slips over the edge it's been hurtling towards and I come as hard as I've ever made myself, yet doesn't even come close to comparing with what his touch did to me before.

Dammit is the only thought running through my mind while I lay there letting my body calm and cool down.

Upon regaining more than a tiny bit of awareness and noticing he hasn't returned, I bound out of the bed and stand there with my arms over my chest as I shout to the room in general. "I don't know what you think I've done, but you need to come talk to me! I'm sorry I lied to you, but I came here to learn about the man my father said I was promised to marry from childhood. That's it! And if you don't want to get to know me, that's fine. I'll get my things and leave. Just tell me what the hell your problem is already and let me go."

Then I climb into the bed and consider everything I can possibly say when he finally dares to face me.

2

OWEN

"You did what?" Simone's question makes me wince as she rises from the couch, placing her hands on her hips and glaring at me since I've just told her about Ramona. "Please tell me you didn't just admit to keeping a woman locked up in a room against her will."

"I can't, but it's complicated."

"No, it isn't. Doesn't matter what you think she or her father has done, you need to free her immediately."

"Fuck, Simone, she's not being treated poorly. I know I've done something I shouldn't, but do plan on letting her go as soon as she tells me what I want to know."

She stares at me for a moment with pursed lips, then sits down with a sigh, crossing her arms over her chest while keeping her eyes locked on mine. "And when will that be?"

"Tomorrow or the next day? It's not like she's

frightened." Not if that little erotic display Ramona gave this morning was anything to go by, at least, but I won't mention that to Simone. Hell, not even Joy knows about it.

For my eyes only, and it will remain that way.

"Of course, she isn't," she says with an exasperated huff. "She's got the moral high ground here. She might've lied, but you've *kidnapped* her, Owen. Seriously now, how do you know she won't report it to the police when you let her go?"

"Not really convincing me to free her with that kind of statement." When she scowls at me again, I put up both my hands in surrender before dropping them while rising. "Fine, fine. I'll go talk to her right now and figure all this shit out. But don't think I'm not pissed off about her duping me. I liked—"

Her gaze softens as she looks up at me when I stop mid-sentence. "You can still like her, Owen. It's not like she's the one who set the fire, she was just a kid. And now she's a woman who came here thinking you might marry her."

"Correct. And who the hell does that, even thirty years ago? Would my father honestly have agreed to such a thing and make some promise he expected me to keep? She's a stranger."

She laughs, shaking her head at me as she stands, and walks close to place a hand on my chest. "Don't be stupid. She wouldn't have been a stranger if you'd grown up together, as I'm sure that's what was intended. You were supposed to be in Russia all this time, not hiding in America." She steps back and raises both brows even as she smiles. "I'm kinda hurt you never told me this before now. What's your birth name?"

"Odin Vasnetsov. And it isn't as if I've been lying, Simone. I haven't used that name in twenty-six years. For all intents and purposes, including legalities, I am Owen Chandler and will remain that way."

"You know I'm not talking about your name."

"Yes, I know." Shoving a hand through my hair, I lean in to kiss the top of her head and exhale hard while taking a step back after so we're no longer touching. "That time of my life is something I've preferred to pretend didn't exist. Clearly, that's no longer an option."

With an affectionate smile, she turns away at the sound of Malik's squeals, bending down to pick him up after he runs into the room and into her arms. "Go on then. You've got some things to figure out and it's time for me to get things done around here."

"Trying to get rid of me," I tease her, wiggling my fingers at Malik as he stares at me over his mother's shoulder. He rewards me with a smile for my efforts even as Simone turns to roll her eyes at me because she damn well knows she doesn't have much to do with all the staff around to help. "All right, I'm going. We'll talk later."

"Yep, call me later."

Heading toward the front door, I pull out my phone and send a quick text message to Joy asking her to make sure Ramona's taken care of with dinner before I arrive home to speak with her.

It's time to figure out what the hell's going on, even if part of me fears the answers to all my questions I've had for so long.

RAMONA'S SITTING ON THE EDGE OF THE BED WITH her legs crossed and hands folded in her lap when I enter the room.

She doesn't even cast a glance my way, keeping her gaze down as I had told her to last night, and instantly making me feel like an asshole for having locked her up in here.

At the same time, it's impossible not to appreciate her luscious naked form, adorned with the silver collar and cuffs that mark her as mine.

Mine. A word with so much power, and before her little speech earlier this morning, a simple word that truly meant nothing without her consent. Yet, I've wanted and desired this woman since the moment my eyes caught a glimpse of her behind the bar and fucking her the other night had only intensified the attraction between us.

Despite what is an unmistakable mutual pull between us, the right thing to do is let her go. But now I'm not so certain and not even the conversation with Simone has convinced me actions are wrong regarding this situation.

See, I thought about everything on the way home. This woman from my home country, the child of the man my father blamed for the house fire, came here to meet and get to know me. Surely her father hadn't sent her here without informing her of his role in the fire that caused my family to flee, had he?

Of course, the only way to determine what she knows is to ask her, and I'm going to have a little fun with her while I still can.

"Pet," I say in an agreeable tone, solidifying my stance to exude dominance by spreading my feet apart a bit and crossing my arms over my chest, and then snap my fingers. "At my feet, now."

She jumps off the bed, hurrying across the room to stand in front of me as bid. Dropping to her knees while placing her hands on her lap, she completes my demand without raising her gaze toward mine even once. The fact she knew I wanted her on her knees must mean Joy gave her directions before my arrival, and her acquiescence without needing reminding pleases me.

She must've really hated being zapped last night.

The thought makes me smile. Uncrossing my arms, my right hand drifts to the top of her head to rest there, and my fingers entangle in her hair.

Pretending I haven't seen the little show she put on this morning, asking the fundamental questions is a good place to start, and deliver my first query in the same pleasant voice. "Why did you come here?"

"To meet you...sir."

Her pause is telling, especially coupled with the squaring of her shoulders, and I wonder how long it will take before she gets angry again. "Your exquisite manners please me. See how easy things are when you follow the rules?"

"Yes, sir."

The sound of her gritting her teeth at the end of her response amuses me, making me grin even as I tighten my hold on her hair in case she's considering trying to do anything. "Why did you want to meet me?"

"Our parents arranged a marriage between us when we were younger, sir, and I got tired of waiting."

"I have never heard of the agreement, but what was the reason for your deception if your visit was as innocent as you say?"

Sniffling she says, "It was harmless, but I realize now I shouldn't have lied. All I wanted was to meet and get to know what kind of man you were before telling you who I really was."

"I can't fathom why you thought to lie instead of just approaching me directly."

"If I'm here because I lied, then I can agree. However, sir, if I'm here because of some other reason, then approaching you directly wouldn't have made much of a difference, would it?"

Of course she's intelligent; she's figured out she isn't here because of her lying to me. What I'm not confident of is whether I should tell her why. "Did your father send you here?"

"No, sir. He didn't want me coming here at all, but at the same time, he's a man who keeps even his oldest promises and that meant I had to something instead of waiting around. Until you either returned home and married me, or told our family it wasn't going to happen, I wasn't free to marry elsewhere."

Incredulous, I release my hold on her hair and take a step back. "You're twenty-nine. You can do whatever you want and that includes marriage."

She doesn't move, but the amusement rings loud and clear as she speaks. "Can I do whatever I want, sir? My current position tells me that isn't exactly correct."

"Smart replies aren't appreciated, pet, and another won't be tolerated."

Even while saying it, I know she won't be able to resist a retort after that and she proves me right, snapping her head up to glare at me as she hisses,

"Won't be tolerated? Or what? You'll make me stand in a corner like a naughty child?"

"Nothing so pedestrian, I assure you." When she merely lifts a brow and smirks as if she doesn't believe I'll do anything, that becomes the moment proving I will is necessary. "Up on your feet, pet."

She doesn't. "Stop calling me that. I'm not your pet."

Stalking forward and crouching down, I grab her upper arms and lift her so she dangles in my grasp. Walking over to the bed, she struggles fruitlessly in my arms to free herself as I take a seat on the edge of it.

Placing her face down across my lap, her hands fly out to steady herself on the ground, and when she kicks her legs, I respond immediately with a sharp smack on the center of her bare ass.

Although she immediately ceases the movement of her legs with a howl, her smart mouth doesn't follow suit, and I know she wishes her head wasn't dangling off my lap so she could scowl at me. "Oh my god, you're spanking me? Talk about juvenile!"

"And yet, here you are, encouraging more delivered with your inability to curb your tongue and address me properly." *Smack!* "Count."

She grits her teeth again before spitting out, "Two."

"Incorrect, pet." *Smack!* "You will start over

since you failed to count from the beginning, and don't forget to address me as directed."

She says nothing, and for a moment, I wonder if she'll put up more a fight before giving in to the inevitable. I tossed in the addressing me while counting to prove a point. Requiring her to follow each slap with a number and a 'sir' is overkill, but I might as well have a bit of fun while she remains in my possession.

Her body remains tense as she finally replies in a whisper. "One, sir."

Gently rubbing her reddening cheeks, I tell her gently, "Relax your body. Tightening your muscles will cause you more discomfort than necessary."

The instant she does, my hand connects with her ass again, and again until she's counted off ten and remains limp in my lap, the sound of her soft weeping filling the surrounding silence.

Lifting her with the intent to comfort, I place her on the bed to better reposition her body to hold her, only she turns away from me and curls into a ball. I should take her in my arms anyway and hold her while she cries, but she won't welcome my touch right now, and doing so may cause more harm than good.

In my experience, the first time can be confusing for some women, especially for one who hasn't been disciplined since they were a child and getting spanked like a child is a difficult adjustment.

After she had ceased resisting, her submission to me in that way had been just as beautiful as the night she begged me to come. And she may not realize how perfect she is for me in that regard, but she will.

For now, I place a hand on her shoulder and stroke down in a soothing manner before saying, "Rest for now, pet. I'll return later."

No smart reply or snide remarks from her as I rise, just a simple whispered, "Yes, sir," through her crying.

Resisting the urge to sit back down and take advantage of her desired docility, I stride to the door after deciding that I can't keep my vow to Simone, or even myself. Let her go? Yes, I know I'll have to, especially since she doesn't seem party to whatever game her father plays, just not yet.

Definitely not today or tomorrow, but when I'm ready, because my anger with this beautiful woman is waning, and in its place is the rekindled desire I wish to explore to the fullest.

3

RAMONA

I DON'T MOVE from my position on the bed for a while. Not because of anything serious, but for the simple fact there's no reason to.

O had held me down and spanked me, and the worst thing is, I can't even be mad at him for it. Did it shock and mortify me that he smacked my ass if I were a child? Yes, and I cried because it was the only way to release my emotions during those moments.

However, that part is the easy one to deal with. What's not so easy to come to terms with is the fact each time his hand met my ass, the sting dissipated fast and left arousal in its wake — especially when I felt him grow hard against my belly from my position across his lap as he delivered each blow.

I don't understand why such an action turned me on. Him? Well, the silver things around my neck and limbs, not to mention his explanation of fulfilling fantasies the night I woke in this bed, make it so the fact spanking me turned him on isn't surprising.

Outside this…whatever this is…I wonder if he prefers to live his life way. If he would want things the way in a relationship too. And it's natural to wonder that considering I've come all this way to find out whether he would honor the marriage agreement or not.

Remembering he said he hadn't heard of the arrangement, I groan because that's my answer, isn't it? What man will want to fulfill a promise he recently learned exists?

I still don't know why he's angry, yet there's no doubt in my mind he will tell me, and probably soon.

When the door opens a while later, I sit up hoping O has returned so we can talk, but instead Joy enters the room with a dinner tray. She walks toward me and stops next to the bed with a quick glance down at me.

"Sit back," she says in a kind voice. "It's better if you remain on a soft surface to eat tonight."

Grateful for the reprieve, it doesn't keep my cheeks from heating at her knowledge of what went on in here, and she puts the tray on my lap once I scoot back against the headboard.

I'm starving, the food smells delicious, and I

smile back at her while picking up the fork to begin eating. "Thank you."

"Once you're done eating, put the tray by the door, and when I return, I'll bring some books for you to read from the other room."

My fork pierces the chicken as she says this, my smile widens in appreciation while bringing the food toward my mouth. "That would be great."

She turns and leaves me to my dinner, as well as wondering when O will return tonight. That is if by later he meant this evening. Not like I have any options except to wait and see, but at least then I'll finally have something to do other than lay in this bed.

HE DOES COME BACK LATER, AND BY THAT, I MEAN after I'm already in bed for the night and trying to rest.

I suppose it's a good thing so many thoughts are going through my head that I haven't fallen asleep, but he must've expected otherwise because even though he comes into the room, he doesn't approach the bed.

Instead, the dim lights of the panel on the wall show his outline leaning back against the door, his head tilted up toward the ceiling.

Just as I wonder where he's been, and whether he's going to come toward me or leave again, he lets out what sounds like a frustrated...growl?... and shoves forward off the door.

Needing answers and not wanting him to leave in case that's what he's going to do, I let out a small cough and roll onto my back to get his attention. It works.

He stops, turning toward the bed, and asks in a soft tone, "Are you awake?"

"I am. Can't sleep for some reason."

Silence for a moment and then the edge in his voice is back when he speaks. "Have you forgotten yourself so soon, pet?"

Swallowing, reminders of what he did earlier and thoughts about what we will do in this near darkness run through my head as I whisper, "No, sir."

"Then perhaps you wish to greet me properly."

"Yes, sir." Sitting up and sliding off the bed, I walk toward him and sink to my knees at his feet, keeping my eyes on the floor even though he wouldn't be able to see if I don't follow that rule in this dim light, and clasp my hands in my lap.

He doesn't touch me right away, standing above me in silence like he's savoring every moment of power he holds over me, and it's hard to keep myself from asking him what's going on in his mind.

When he finally does, he only rests his hand on top of my head and says, "I believe you came here with pure intentions, but it leaves me with questions you won't be able to answer."

"I'm sorry, sir."

"You have nothing to apologize for. Your father is a different matter, however."

"My father?"

"He let you come here to fulfill a promise he must've known my dad wouldn't have upheld, especially considering the hand yours had in our family fleeing the country."

Frowning, it takes everything I have to stay still and not move my head to look up at him. "I don't follow. What does your father not keeping the promise have to do with mine helping your family get new identities and escape safely?"

"I'm afraid you're mistaken," he announces in the saddest tone I've heard him use since we met, his hand leaving my head as he takes a step back. "My father maintained your father's role in burning down our house until the day he died."

"What?" Reeling from this, I shake my head adamantly before realizing he can't see it. "No. That's wrong. Your father was wrong. My father would never—"

He interrupts with a harshly spoken, "Are you calling my father a liar, pet?"

Flinching, my heart drops into my stomach, making me feel sick at realizing what he must've thought of finding out my identity, and understanding his reaction completely. "N-no, sir.

M-my father has spoken of yours through the years with me. We discussed you all the time. I told you, he wouldn't let me break the promise to marry you. W-why would he do that if…if…"

"If he knew it would never happen? I don't know, but my father would have had no reason to accuse your father if it weren't true."

Tears spring to my eyes. There's so much I want to say, but what would be the point? His father is dead; we can't ask him why he thought that. And my father…why would my father lie to me? What purpose would he have had in sending me here if he had known?

It doesn't make any sense, but that doesn't matter. This can only mean one thing.

"Are you letting me go then, sir?"

"I will be, yes."

That's all he says even though he continues to stand above me without moving.

I want to ask when? And is this it? But mostly, I want to know why he doesn't walk out and leave because the truth is out, and nothing good is going to happen between us now. Too much history and pain, even I know that.

Yet, what better than right this moment to take a chance, if only for one more opportunity to touch him? And have him touch me because I loved it so much. What do I have to lose?

Rising slowly, I get to my feet and take a step

toward him, until my naked body barely brushes his clothed one.

He sucks in a breath, his hand coming to cover mine when they find his belt buckle as he asks, "What are you doing?"

"I think what I'm doing is obvious."

"No." He grabs my hand and removes it, stepping back while clearing his throat. "You didn't come here on your own, which means—"

Consent. Of course. Good thing that's an easy thing to fix.

"Tell me I'm free, then." Angry even though his reason for denying me is legitimate, I cut him off and step closer again, grabbing his shirt in my fist so he can't back off again. "And follow it up by asking me to stay."

Unable to see much of his face, I can't watch it to get an idea of what he's thinking, but I take him not trying to pull away as a good sign.

The desire to urge him to give me what I want makes me bold. "Free me, sir, and then show me what you would do to me once I'm here willingly."

For a moment I fear he will refuse me.

Then, one of his hands finds its way to the back of my head, resting there as he brings his mouth close to mine and murmurs, "You're free to leave, pet, but you'll need to prove you wish to remain here for the night."

Letting that statement wash over me, I

acknowledge his message silently: tonight only. Nothing else…and he's giving me a choice.

His hand drops away when I step back wordlessly, and the sound of his sharp intake of breath is everything I could wish for when I make my decision for the night. Placing both hands flat on his shirt-covered stomach, I slowly sink to my knees before him. My hands slide to his belt where they stop, poised to unbuckle it, but waiting for an objection.

When he remains silent, I undo his belt before the button on his pants, sliding the zipper down slow and teasing before slipping my hand inside. His cock is hard and thick as I wrap my hand around it, amazed that he's so big my fingers don't come close to touching as I free him from the restriction of his clothing.

The long, guttural groan of pleasure he makes when I lick and then take the tip of him in my mouth is accompanied by his hands returning to rest on my head. At first, he keeps them there, occasionally flexing his hands to grab my hair before letting go while letting me take him into my mouth at my own pace.

I don't get far before he tightens his hold, tilting my head back a little as he gives in to the passion between us, taking control like we both want him to anyway. "Drop your hands, pet, and open wide."

The moment my hands leave his dick, he

shoves himself deep into my mouth, keeping my head immobile in his grasp. Unprepared, he pulls back as I gag and says with a soft laugh, "Relax your throat and breathe through your nose."

Repeating the motion a second later, my lips stretch around him as he fills my mouth and, this time, it's easier since I relax my throat as he instructed. He moves out and back in, making sure to go all the way and hold his position for more than a few seconds before withdrawing.

And while I expected the soft sounds of pleasure from him, I hadn't thought my own body would respond to giving a man oral this way, the wetness between my legs growing with each thrust of his cock.

Gliding a hand down my stomach, I don't get too far when he pauses with his cock to the back of my throat and growls, "Don't you dare touch yourself without my permission."

Deliberately ignoring him just to see what happens, I slide two fingers between the slippery lips and stick them inside myself, gasping around his cock while lifting my hips into the motion.

He pulls out of my mouth and releases me so abruptly I'm unprepared to catch myself; if it weren't for him scooping me up in his arms, I would've hit the floor thanks to my crouched position. But he does, placing me stomach down over his shoulder as he stalks to the bed, and tosses me onto the center of it.

Within a few seconds, he adjusts my body so I'm face down on the bed and my arms are spread wide above my head after he attaches the cuffs to the headboard. Climbing on the bed, he positions my body so my knees are bent and my ass is in the air, then covers my body with his as he leans in close to my ear.

"I remember how much you like to run your mouth, so let's take care of that right now, hm?" He pushes something round against my mouth and the battle of wills doesn't last long as he gags me, snapping it around my head while I attempt to futilely push it out with my tongue. "If you need me to stop, you just shake one of your arms and it will rattle the chain. Shake it once to tell me you understand, twice to stop right now."

When I shake it once, because there's no way I want him to stop now when my body is so ready for him, he presses a kiss just below my ear and whispers, "Good girl. Don't shake it again unless you want me to stop."

The warmth of his body leaves my back cold as he gets off me, cutting off my moan of protest with the sudden plunge of his cock into my pussy and his fingers digging into my hips. Keeping himself deep, one of his hands moves to the front of my body and between my legs, two fingers finding my clit as he chuckles low.

"You can't talk or disobey me this way, but the

plus side is you and your delicious body can come as many times as you want, pet."

Slowly pulling back, he sinks in leisurely, his two fingers resting on either side of my clit in a perpetual tease as he keeps the pace until I buck my hips into his seeking release. As many times as I want? Bullshit. And his naughty snicker every time I move my hips tells me he's aware of what his torture is doing to me.

Then, both of us groan in unison as he thrusts hard and deep, but that mixed with his fingers suddenly pinching my clit sets off my first orgasm of the night. His pace remains nearly the same maddening pattern after that, slowly eliciting a second and eventually a third orgasm from me before my body feels sated and boneless.

Leaving my body after the last one, he moves to undo the chains attached to my cuffs, removes the gag from my mouth, and rolls me onto my back before climbing between my legs. Lazily wrapping my arms around his neck and my legs around his hips, he enters me again with a groan and seeks entrance to my mouth with a nip of his teeth on my lips.

He kisses me with slow, intense thrusts of his tongue meant to match those of his cock inside me, and when he finally comes, he does with a husky groan as he stills. Quick to remove his weight, he rolls to lie on his back and takes me with him, his heart beating fast beneath where my head rests on his chest.

Nothing more is spoken between us because we each drift off before long, and when morning comes, I greet it alone just like every other day since my arrival.

Somehow that simple fact makes me feel alone more than ever and it's not long before this day turns that feeling into an abrupt yet expected reality.

4

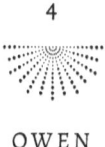

OWEN

I COULD'VE WOKEN up next to her, but I decided not to as the better course of action. Her expression is filled with sadness as she lays in bed this morning, making my guilt and self-reproach rise fast because I shouldn't have slept with her again.

Sex with Ramona last night? Fantastic. Better than the first time, and I'm sure it would only get more so if we kept fucking each other.

However, that's not going to happen, because she'll be heading home by the end of the day.

She had choices last night. I gave her the freedom that would've been given to her today anyway and she desired me as much as I had her. So it's a mystery to me as to why things feel wrong when I merely gave into the mutual desire between us.

Perhaps not acknowledging the why is better.

After everything's said and done, no amount of anything — not even liking this beautiful and intelligent woman — will change the past or all the obstacles here in the present.

Standing up and walking out of the video room, Joy's heading down the hall toward me, and frowns the moment she catches sight of my neutral expression.

Of course, she knows what I want, and her shoulders droop even as she crosses her arms over her chest with a sharpness that declares her irritation. "I thought after last night—"

Holding up a hand, I cut her off and stalk past her, taking the stairs downstairs with Joy on my heels. "You were mistaken. Please see to it she's compensated for her work at the bar and her flight home is taken care of. She needs to be on her way back this evening."

"Goddamnit, Owen," she hisses, grabbing at my arm as we reach the bottom of the steps and holding on even though I continue walking. "Fucking stop, right now, and talk to me."

Whirling on her, I have to respect the fact she doesn't back down, even though I'm in her face. That's the one thing I've always loved about Joy; even when she knows she's going to lose, she doesn't back down. "About what, hm? I love you, Joy, and you're my family, but this? This isn't your fucking business, and you need to do as I ask because that's your *job*, remember?"

Her eyes grow watery as she responds softly, "Your well-being is always my concern, and will always come before the work I do for you."

Flinching, and feeling like the asshole I'm well aware of being, I place my hands on her shoulders and shake my head. "I can't do this, all right? If she were anyone else, we wouldn't be having this conversation."

"But you care for her, Owen. Why does it matter that much when she had nothing to do with it? You can't just send her away like she's—"

I cut her off by taking a step back, my words sharp and angry. "Joy, we will not discuss this any further. You will make sure she's gone before I return this evening and I don't want to hear of it again."

Pivoting before she can say anything further, I walk to the front door and out of it, getting into the car and instructing the driver to just go with no particular destination in mind.

Somewhere, anywhere, is better than being here where the temptation to forget everything for another few moments alone with the last woman in the world I should feel something for hounds me.

THE WOMAN MUST HAVE A HONING DEVICE.

Otherwise, how has Sally managed to walk

into the one place in town rarely frequented by me, and spot me within seconds?

The good news is I've been nursing my first drink for a while now. The bad news is the same because up until arriving here getting drunk seemed like a great idea, yet the idea of drinking to oblivion, as usual, isn't appealing.

She heads my way with a blinding smile, only to slip into the booth across from me instead of 'accidentally' falling into my lap in her customary manner.

Stunned at the change of pace, it takes a moment before I notice something about her different, and really study her. The thorny woman I've come to know is nowhere to be seen, replaced by one with bright eyes, a dazzling smile, and softened countenance.

It's the sort of expression I've seen more recently in my life than ever before and with a sardonic smile, I lift my glass in a toast to her. "Congratulations are in order, I suspect."

She nods, wiggling the fingers of her left hand to display the gorgeous diamond on it, and then clasps her hands in her lap. "He proposed last night."

"I didn't know you were seeing anyone, Sally."

"Like we ever talked about anything personal, Owen. Although now that we're engaged, he requests my sessions with you stop altogether."

"He knew?"

"Yeah. Of course." She rolls her eyes, reminding me the bratty part of her I've always liked is still in there and sighs in that dreamy way girls do when they've lost their damn minds over someone. "Told me he understood my needs as a single woman, but in the next step of our relationship, he would be taking over the role-play."

I don't even try to understand this and honestly, I don't want to. It's Sally's relationship and, per my remark to Joy earlier, none of my fucking business.

"Well, if you're happy, then that's all that matters."

"Thank you." She glances away for a moment with a dreamy look then back at me with a lift of one singular and all too familiar naughty brow. "You look like shit, just so you know."

"Wow." When she smirks, I finish off my drink and set it on the table with a small clink. "I don't look like shit. I'm dressed the same as always."

"I'm not talking about your clothing and you know it." She points at her own eyes and teases with an amused laugh. "Didn't take you for the crying type."

My eyes are red from sleeping poorly, not from crying, and she damn well knows it.

Her eyes darken in an anticipation she can't

hide, even if she's no longer free to indulge after I lean toward her with a calculated smile. "Think you're safe from getting put over my knee for that smart mouth of yours? Think again."

Licking her lips and blushing, she opens her mouth, only to snap it shut when the waitress stops next to the table. When she merely orders water instead of her standard 'one drink at a minimum' I don't even bother trying to hide my surprise.

"Don't even," she says with a pointed finger at me, acting as if that's all it takes to make sure I won't comment. "I'm trying to cut back on my drinking."

"Another request of the soon-to-be husband?"

"You're being a jackass," she comments with a flip of her hair, "but yeah, actually. Some people actually don't mind giving a little if it means they get what they need in the end."

"Sobriety?"

Another roll of her eyes as the waitress sets the water down before walking away after a quick shake of my head lets her know I don't want another.

"A baby, sir," she continues with marked sarcasm at the last word. "I want marriage and a family, all right? So yeah, I think drinking a lot less will be conducive to that."

"I didn't take you for the motherly type." When she glares at me, I reach across the table and cover her hand with mine, not letting my amusement at how a slight change in the dynamic between us can change how we interact instantly. "I meant I never knew you wanted children, that's all."

"It's okay." Slipping her hand out from under mine, she smiles briefly before picking up her glass and taking a sip of the water. "Bound to happen with you trying as hard as you can to avoid anything personal, huh?"

"Hazard of the job. Play time is just that, play time. Any blurring of the lines could lead to trouble I'm not interested in participating in."

"So you've said. It sure is one way to keep yourself from ever having to get serious with anyone." When I frown at her, she snickers and twirls a piece of hair around one finger before asking, "What happened to that obnoxious woman?"

The abrupt change of subject makes me blink in confusion. "Who?"

"The self-righteous cock-blocker you hired. Nobody seems to know where she went."

I don't even try to hold back my laughter at the way Sally's referring to Ramona, but do manage to merely snicker before clearing my throat. "Something came up, so she's heading home."

"Too bad. I saw the way you watched her that night even when you were drunk off your ass."

"Her refusing to let you take me home with

you was rather amusing, even you have to admit that."

"Yeah. It's a good story for sure." At the sound of a lyrical ding, she digs into her purse and pulls out her phone, her lips curving into a brilliant smile telling me exactly who's texting before she looks at me again. "He's off work early, so I've gotta go now. Don't drink too much okay? You're too easily taken advantage of."

Both of us laugh as she scoots out of the booth, and after tossing enough cash on the table to cover my drink and tip, I decide it's time for me to leave as well.

Standing up, I offer my elbow to her, which she takes with a nod after I say, "I'll walk you out."

Once we reach her car, she unlocks the door and opens it before turning back to catch me off guard with a hug. When she pulls back to find me staring down at her, she steps up on tiptoe to peck my cheek before stepping back with a cheeky wink. "See you around, Owen."

For a few minutes after she drives off I stand there staring after her car, glad she's seemed to find someone who makes her happy and will fulfill her needs, only to realize this must be what closure feels like.

Pulling my phone out of my pocket, the glaring digits of the clock on my home screen declaring it past nine p.m. makes me release a frustrated growl before I shove it back into my pocket.

It's too late.

Joy would've sent Ramona on her way now, and instead of telling myself I'm an idiot for thinking it was better to send her away without even saying goodbye, I decide to have that second drink after all and head back to the restaurant.

By the time I arrive home, it's four in the morning, and the last thing I expect is for Joy to be waiting for me.

Yet there she is, practically glaring daggers at me from where she sits in front of the fireplace nursing a drink in her hand and points at the sofa with a twist of her lips. "Take a seat."

"Only if you promise not to throw your glass at me."

At her disgusted scoff, I take a seat in the other chair instead and sigh, waiting for her unavoidable and completely deserved lecture.

It never arrives. Instead, she finishes her drink and rolls the glass between her hands without glancing my way as she asks, "You know why I stayed working with you all these years, Owen?"

"I assume your reasons were many, one of which is the fact I wasn't as much of a heartless asshole as I've become, no doubt."

Her lips curve in the firelight before she flattens her mouth out with a highly deserved disapproval that outweighs her brief amusement. "After your mother had died, you were in a lot of pain, but what I liked about you most was your attitude. You didn't let her death take you off your path or divert you from getting what you wanted out of life. You were amazing, which is why I chose to stay around and work for you. I thought the way you enjoyed life was truly inspiring."

Rising, she walks toward me and holds the glass out, waiting for me to take it before pointing at it. "See that? That's how you appear to me right now — empty and aching for something to fill the hole inside you. And for years now you've gone after what you've wanted, trying to do exactly that, but it never lasts long."

"Joy—"

She lifts her chin, crossing her arms over her chest and glancing in the direction of the door before frowning at me again. "You always go after what you want. Why, this one time when you know you've found someone special, have you decided not to do whatever you can to hold onto it?"

"You know why." Wiggling the glass in my grip, I sit it on the end table and stand up, letting out an agitated sigh. "She's the daughter of the man my father thought betrayed him, and neither she nor I know who told the fucking truth, but that doesn't mean everything should be forgotten. My loyalty is, and will always be, to my family."

"I'm not telling you to forget," she whispers with watery eyes, wiping at her cheek when a tear escapes down it. "I'm saying you need to realize there's nothing you can do and be with a woman who fulfills you in a way I've never seen before. Or, if you can't do that, then you fight for her while also striving to uncover the truth, and be with her anyway."

Knowing she can't understand, because she's never had such a betrayal happen in her family, I merely shake my head and ask the most important question of the evening. "Is she gone, Joy?"

"Yes. For many hours now. I contemplated disobeying you, but despite everything, I know forcing your hand isn't the way to go."

"Thank you." Moving to stand in front of her, she lets me drawn her into an embrace and returns it with a sniffle. "Now, I'm exhausted and heading to bed. You should as well."

"I'm still mad at you," she mumbles, dropping her arms and giving me a sad look as she stares up at my face. "See you in the morning."

Kissing the top of her head, I release her and say, "Good night, Joy. Love ya."

"I love you too, but right now, I don't like you."

She walks out of the room without another word, and the only thing running through my head as I head to bed is how much I don't like myself right now either.

Especially since my loyalty isn't going to keep my bed warm at night with the one woman who quickly became the perfect person for the chronically empty role, leaving me wondering if the chance will ever come around again.

5

RAMONA

"It's time to leave."

Out of all the things I expect Joy to say when she walks into my room later the next day, that definitely isn't one of them.

Closing the book I was reading, I set it next to me on the bed before giving Joy my full attention, both eyebrows furrowing in confusion. "I'm sorry?"

She takes a step closer, clasping her hands in front of her while looking me straight in the face for the first time she began taking care of me on a daily basis, and smiles softly at me. "I said, you are leaving. Owen's asked me to get your things, take off the cuffs, and see you are headed home safely tonight."

"Oh? He couldn't tell me himself?"

"No." She shakes her head at the same time and lowers her gaze. "He doesn't wish to have any further contact with you."

Disappointment squeezes my heart and makes my stomach queasy even though I understand completely. He thinks my father set the fire and it will remain a wedge between us because as I asked him, why would my papa say he helped him leave all these years if it weren't true? Yes, he didn't want me to come here to see O, but he's always talked about keeping the marriage promise.

There's no reason he would've done that knowing I would eventually find out he tried to kill his best friend.

Something stinks here, but O wouldn't listen to my protests, and now he wants me gone. It hurts. After all, the sex last night had been incredible and I stupidly hoped he might realize everything that happened all those years ago doesn't have anything to do with us now.

But maybe I'm wrong. Maybe it does and I'm just too close to the situation to understand. Well, he can have what he wants, because it's clear he won't be persuaded otherwise. I have no leverage to wage a fight about this and I'm ready to go home just so I'm far away from here before breaking down.

Standing up, I hold out my arms and say in a defeated whisper, "Okay. Thanks."

Not long after she removes the cuffs and collar, she returns my clothes to me and leads me out of the house.

Handing me an envelope as we stop next to

the car, she maintains eye contact as she says, "Your flight leaves in four hours. Your ticket is inside as are your earnings. The car will take you to your place and then to the airport."

Although I don't need the money, I don't want to offend her so I take the envelope and shove it in my pocket before turning away to open the door, only to glance back to find her frowning at me. "What's wrong?"

"I thought it would go differently," she admits with a twist of her lips. "The moment he knew who you were, he fought with how much he liked you over what happened in the past, and I thought he would choose you. Foolish of me after knowing him all these years."

I want to reassure her, to let her know it's okay he can't let it go, except we both know it isn't. And perhaps rightly so. Someone robbed him and his family of their feelings of safety, changing his whole life with their actions.

"It's all right." She takes the door handle and nods at me to indicate I should get inside. "You should go now. Take care, Miss Dorokhova."

"You too, Joy." *Take care of him.*

After I'm seated she shuts the door and the car takes me toward my apartment. The drive takes a while but once we arrive, I head upstairs, glancing around to make sure I've got everything while swiping at the tears slipping down my cheeks. My trip here had been filled with hope that I would finally get what I waited all these years for.

How foolish of me. Now I'm going home with even less than I came here with, including the tiny part of my heart I foolishly gave to a man who doesn't want to ever see me again.

It's not right, but I turn and walk out of the apartment without a backward glance, making sure to bury any other emotions about this all deep where I hope to never deal with them again.

A CAR SENT BY MY FATHER PICKS ME UP FROM THE Aeroport Pulkovo, and after the long flight, I fall asleep in the car within a few minutes of heading toward home.

Woken up by the driver tapping gently on the window, he waits outside patiently as I sit up and rub my eyes. Feeling refreshed from having slept the whole way here — a good thing since I would need it to deal with my father in my already heightened emotional state — I open up the door and take his proffered hand to step out.

"Your father said to let you know he wishes to speak with you upon your arrival," he says while shutting the door. "Glad to have you back, Miss Dorokhova."

I wish my feelings on being home were the same. And although my trip wasn't that long, it's shocking to realize how used to speaking English I've become and take a deep breath before responding to him in our native tongue. "Thank you, Viktor."

Heading inside, I walk toward my father's office, all the things O told me whirling around in my head. Doubts about my papa's honesty, something I never thought I would be questioning, have me wanting to go to my room instead of speaking with him tonight.

But if I don't go to him he'll come to me so, with a sigh, I stop outside his office, run a hand through my hair, and knock on the barely open door.

"Enter." Stopping just inside and clasping my hands together, after he bids me entrance, my father lifts his head and smiles upon seeing me, placing his pen on the desk before sitting back. "Ah, *kotenok*, you've returned."

He says that as if I hadn't called before getting on the plane and gestures for me to sit. Getting up, he pours two drinks and hands me one before sitting down again, waiting for me to speak.

"Viktor said you wanted to talk, Papa?"

"Tell me how your trip went."

Not a question, but a demand, because my father doesn't ask. He says what he wants and it's easier to answer him than ever because I have questions. "It went differently than I expected.

Odin said he didn't know about the agreement and then I came home."

No need to get into the details, many of which are none of his business, and make sure to shrug so he thinks nothing of significance happened.

He studies me, staring at me over the edge of his glass before taking a sip and setting it down on the desk with a confident smile. "I figured this might happen, *kotenok*, but don't fret. I have made alternative plans for you."

My head rears back at words I wasn't prepared to hear at all. "Sorry? What plans?"

"Marriage. It is no surprise my old friend didn't tell his son, as he said they had no intentions of ever returning to his homeland, but as you know, I am a man of my word and thought he would change his mind. Now with the knowledge you've brought me, I will accept it as truth, and our family may make new plans for the future."

Clenching the glass, I stare at him for a moment before dropping my gaze as my sight grows misty and keep my voice steady while my heart feels crushed in my chest. "And what plans have you made for me?"

"You will marry Maksim. He is a good man, and although I know he wouldn't be your first choice, he is a good fit for the family and business. I know he will take excellent care of you, and it's my utmost priority that my daughter is well cared for when I am gone."

Lifting my eyes to his, I let him see my pain in a way I never have before, but he doesn't even blink at the tears on my cheeks. "Am I to have no say in this, Papa? What if I don't wish to marry him? Or anyone?"

"You will not be dramatic, *malyutka*. You've always known you would marry a man of my choosing and there will be no more waiting. The wedding shall take place between you and Maksim in four weeks time." He stands up and comes around the desk, staying just to my left and leaning against it. Reaching out, he takes my hand in his and gives it a gentle squeeze. "I know you are shocked, but he is a good man, yes?"

"He is." It's not a lie to agree because Maksim is a good person; I just don't believe he is the man for me. Not my first choice? More like my never choice...if I were being given one, that is. "Will you tell me something, Papa?"

"Of course."

"Have you ever lied to me? About anything, at all, in my life?"

His brows furrow, which I've learned over the years means he's trying to understand why the question was asked, and tilts his head a little to the side. "You are questioning my integrity."

"I am asking you a question I need you to answer."

His eyes search mine, but nothing changes in his from his usual severity, and he doesn't even need to say the words for me to know he hasn't lied to me. "I have never lied to you, *kotenok*. I can hardly expect honesty from you and others if there is no truth from me, hm?"

"Of course, Papa." Smiling at him, I put my glass down and rub at my burning eyes. "It was a long trip and I'm tired."

He releases my hand and walks back to his seat, sitting down before leveling the serious expression I know by heart at me. "If you wish to say something to me about your trip, I would hear it now."

Meaning he wants to know why I asked him that question, but I won't tell him. Odin sent me away and wants nothing to do with me or my family; there's no reason to tell my father of anything. Odin's father had been mistaken for some unknown reason, and maybe if he hadn't been, things would've been different.

The thought alone makes my heart hurt all over again.

Rising, I decide to appease him with a simple statement that says everything and nothing simultaneously. "My trip taught me that my reality is different from that of others, and because of it, I won't disappoint you. If you desire for me to marry Maksim, then I will, but only because I know him as decent and don't want for you to feel troubled."

"You will find happiness with him, *kotenok*. If

not now, then one day, especially with a marriage based on the friendship you two already possess." He picks up his pen and points toward the ceiling with it. "Your return will please your mother. She missed you."

While I love my mother and am sure she missed me, I'm more convinced she's thrilled a wedding is in my future and can't wait to plan it.

So, with a final smile at him, the large part of me that had an experience show me the joy a real connection with someone might bring me heads to my bedroom to cry for everything I will never have now.

Then, tomorrow morning, the dutiful daughter I am will wake up with dry eyes to do what is best for my family...even if it breaks my heart to think of marrying a man who doesn't make me feel anything more than brotherly toward him.

MAKSIM DOESN'T WASTE ANY TIME COMING TO see me.

I haven't even been home twenty-four hours, and fifteen minutes before lunch he's welcomed inside by mama, who laughs at something he said as they walk into the living room.

When he takes the seat next to me, she walks back out with a remark about checking on the food, which she doesn't need to do since we have a private chef. An obvious ploy to let my future husband have a few private moments alone with me, and one he takes advantage of as he moves a bit closer, taking both my hands in his.

"I am glad you have returned, *malyshka*. I believe we have much to discuss."

Nodding, because of course my father would've informed him of my agreement immediately, I gently tug my hands from his hold and clasp them in my lap with a frown. "Was this your idea, Maksim? If so, I'm quite unhappy at having my life decided for me when I wasn't even here to object."

"You know no one does anything your papa doesn't want them to do," he replies, dancing around the question with a smile that might work with a woman who isn't me before sighing at my deepened scowl. "No, *malyshka*, not my idea. Your papa's aware of how I feel and knows I will take good care of you as my wife. It will make me happy to be your husband."

This isn't the first time he's called me little one and it's hard not to smile at that. He is not much taller than me, although he has a solid build and I know from experience he can pick me up with little effort on his part. But even with his dark, choppy short hair, which is usually tousled from him shoving his fingers through it, dark green-blue eyes, and clean-shaven masculine features, there's no attraction between us — at least on my end.

How the hell I'm supposed to suddenly feel something for this man, who has been my friend for many years, that my Papa wants me to marry and start a family with?

I know many girls in my shoes wouldn't even hesitate for a good man like him, and perhaps my pickiness is the problem after pinning my hopes on the mysterious man across the ocean all these years. But if O wanted me, he wouldn't have sent me away, and I'm torn between doing my duty by marrying Maksim or spending my days hoping O will change his mind.

And if a man couldn't even bother to say goodbye to a woman he had slept with before he sent her away, all my common sense tells me him changing his mind isn't likely. My heart doesn't want to listen, but maybe for once I need to ignore it and do the smart, dutiful thing.

"I don't feel the same way about you as you feel about me," I begin softly, only for him to cut me off with a gentle press of his thumb against my lips.

"You may turn me down if you wish, but my hope is you will give me a chance to show you how good our life together would be." His hand moves to cup the left side of my face, his thumb moving to caress my cheek, and when he leans in toward me to whisper against my mouth, I freeze in place. "I'm going to kiss you now, *malyshka*."

Caught in his hold, he doesn't wait for my agreement, and for the first time since we met as children I'm aware of the power he can exert over me if he wants to. His lips cover mine while his free arm steals around my waist and pulls me toward him, my hands coming up to land flat on his chest to prevent our bodies from touching too much.

For a few seconds, with our closed mouths pressed against one another, no part of me reacts to this intimacy with him just as I thought would happen. But then his hand slides toward my neck, fingers gliding into the hair at the nape of my neck as he reaches his destination, and those same fingers snap shut with a large chunk of my hair trapped in them.

Coupled with the sudden nip of his teeth on my lower lip, my tiny gasp at the thrill his unexpected manhandling sparks in me is all he needs to take advantage with his tongue, using his firm hold to declare his desire with a slow exploratory kiss.

I curl my hands into fists while slamming my eyes shut, clutching his shirt in my grip as he angles my head to deepen the kiss, and admit I'm wrong as his passion calls out to my own. But it's not enough because slowly a feeling of betrayal seeps through and when I recognize it as disloyalty against O, I can't rip my lips away from Maksim's fast enough.

His face fills confusion when I force myself to look at him, both of us breathing hard in the aftermath even as he drops his hands from around me.

"I can't." Tears fill my eyes, the desire to cry worsening when his eyes grow soft with empathy for my obvious pain, and the urge to get away intensifies. "This is all wrong."

"Ah, *malyshka*," he says in a voice meant to soothe me, lifting a hand toward my face once again. "It's not wrong, just different, and everything will be good between us before long."

Anger mixes with my own turmoil at the blurring of what I always thought was the hard line between us, and without thinking of the consequences, I lash out by slapping his hand away from my face. His eyes widen at the show of temper from me he's never witnessed before, and unsure what to do with it, he yanks my body toward his again as his expression relaxes despite his shock.

"Let me go!"

Before he can even open his mouth, I shove him hard and when that doesn't get him to release, my palms connects with his face in a slap I'm sure my mama will hear in the kitchen.

But I'm mistaken in thinking that will work because it doesn't, and something on my face must clue Maksim into the emotional pain taking over because he wraps me tight in his arms despite my reluctance and tucks my head into the crook of his shoulder.

He whispers sweet words into my ear as my struggle against his hold slowly turns into me clinging to him, softly sobbing courtesy of the inevitable breakdown's arrival, and my acceptance of things changing forever whether I want them to or not.

6

OWEN

"I've come to tell you, again, that you've made the wrong decision."

Joy shuts my office door and leans against it, her expression one she's worn more this week than all the years I've known her: disappointment. She's barely spoken to me since our conversation the night I sent Ramona home, however, so I've known this moment would arrive eventually, and it has.

Choosing to misunderstand her is the way to go since I hope to avoid having another discussion about the whole situation I don't want to think about again. "I imprisoned an innocent woman and rectified my misjudgment by freeing her and sending her home on my dime. I would say I've corrected my error and done the right thing."

"You will go after her."

"Will I, Joy? Sorry if you're upset but, as I said before, you've no say in this."

"Yes, I do." She walks closer and puts her arm on my shoulder after reaching my side. "She is your future and you know it. You must go after her and claim her."

"Fucking hell, Joy, she's not a piece of property."

"Of course, she isn't, but wouldn't you rather she be yours than have something bad happen to her?"

At that, I jerk my gaze to hers and glare. "What the hell are you going on about?"

"Everything's changed. You told her the truth — your truth — and she's told you hers. Which is the correct one? What if the truth isn't what either of you believe? How do you know she isn't in danger now that you've potentially exposed someone's secrets to her?"

I haven't thought such a thing, and for good reason, including the obvious. "You believe I haven't thought about this, Joy? Wondering to myself...would her father honestly have allowed her to come here if he had been behind the fire? No, he wouldn't have, right? A smart man who wanted to hide something would've stopped her coming to find me if such were the case. She said her father knew where my family has been all this time — if he actually wanted to get rid of us, wouldn't he have taken care of us and told her we weren't alive?"

"My thoughts precisely." Joy lifts a brow, giving

me the 'look' that indicates she thinks I'm being dense. "But think, if her father knew, then somebody else knew. Or now knows, at the very least, and Ramona could be in danger if she starts questioning everything she's ever been told."

"You believe her father divulging my location has put her in danger? Am I not the one who barely escaped a fire set by someone with the intention to kill my family and me?"

"Of course, but it's obvious — to me, at least — that she came here thinking you would honor the...well, the betrothal. And she seemed shocked by the allegations of her father involved with the fire, which means..."

Oh, fuck. My mind fills in the blanks, which should've been obvious from the beginning, and I slam down my hand on the desk. "Which means her father doesn't know mine believed he set the fire."

"Exactly!" I hate when Joy crows with righteousness, but she deserves to in this case, because my anger at being duped has gotten in the way of everything — including my common sense, it seems. "She says her father helped your family flee the country, but you told me your dad said someone else came to his aid. Do you know who it was?"

"No, it was ages ago. All I recall is him ranting about how he couldn't believe such a good friend would do something so evil." Even while saying this, I open the drawer to my right, searching through it for the key to the storage unit where I put all my father's things when he died until I could sort through them, and shove it in my pocket once I've found it. "I'll search through his belongings. Maybe he'll have kept something useful."

"Go on. I'll keep an eye on things here."

Standing up, I lean in to kiss her cheek, and then walk over to grab my coat off the rack before leaving without another word.

SHIT.

There are minimal papers in my father's things and none of them tell me what I want to know. After several hours of digging, I'm frustrated and wondering why the fuck this even matters.

Ramona is gone. I doubt her father will let anyone hurt her. Hell, from the way she explained it, her father would marry her to someone else if the agreement between us wasn't kept.

She might even be married or on her way to marrying someone already, and why the fuck am I even thinking about this? I had liked her in spite of her parentage and I'm sure she wanted me, but it's not as if we knew each other well enough to love one another. Hell, we just fucking met a week ago.

The look on her face when Joy said she was leaving, though…

Yes, after coming home drunk the night I asked Joy to make sure Ramona went back to Russia, I watched the video of it. Typically I do that with all the women who play here with me, but shouldn't have done it this time. Watching Joy tell her I wanted nothing more to do with her made forgetting her confused, sad expression quite impossible.

If nothing else, I should've said goodbye, and if I ever see her again, apologizing for my behavior is first on my list. Fucking her senseless, the second.

What?

Goddammit, no. Joy's lecture repeats itself in my mind, but I'm not going back to Russia. I'm not Odin Vasnetsov and haven't been for over two decades; nothing will change that after all this time.

However, I will do my best to figure out who set the fire if it wasn't Ramona's father, and hopefully, find a way to take care of whoever was behind it because being and feeling safe are important things. In the end, even if Ivan Dorokhov set the fire, his daughter doesn't deserve to pay for it.

My hand smacking into something at the bottom of a box distracts me from my thoughts. Taking it out while wondering how I missed this box the first time around, I set it on top of the boxes piled next to me before opening it up and grimace at only finding a haphazard stack of pictures inside.

I almost close it until the sight of my name scrawled on the back of one near the top catches my attention. Grabbing the stack, I flick through them one by one and realize my father kept every picture from the years we lived in Russia together as a family in this box.

Pictures I had no idea he had until this moment.

There are plenty of them. Me. My mother and me. All three of us beaming into the camera. My father and Ivan. Ivan with his daughter cradled in his arms as he grins at the camera, her mother standing there with the same happiness all over her face while staring at Ramona.

Then, the last one, with little three-year-old Ramona standing next to me, holding my hand while staring up at my face with an angry scowl instead of the camera as I am, my own expression bewildered and annoyed.

Shutting my eyes, I pinch the bridge of my nose as the long-lost memory resurfaces.

"Odin!" My mama stands there with hands on her hips, nodding at the little girl hanging shyly in the doorway. "Take her hand and bring her this way. We must take a picture to mark today. One day you two will marry and this photo will be there to show when it was decided."

I don't want to take a picture or hold Ramona's hand, but it helps that she's not dirty. Walking over, I take her hand in mine like mama said and walk back over to where I stood before, my mother aiming the camera at us.

Ramona tugs on my hand and when I look down at her, she just smiles at me and says, "I like pictures."

"That's nice." I don't know why she wants photos of us together, but I wish mama would take it already so I can go play with my friends. "I don't."

"Why?"

"Look this way, you two."

"I no like you," she whispers when I don't answer, even though she holds my hand tighter. "Pictures nice, but not you."

"I don't care."

My mother snaps the picture the moment I turn toward her, and without waiting for her to tell me we're finished, I yank my hand from Ramona's and run out of the house.

The sound of something tumbling to the ground makes me jump and, with a curse at the unwanted memory, I begin to shove the pictures back into the damn box when a little white card catches my eyes.

It's old, dirty and crinkled, with nothing more than a number scrawled on it. Shoving it into my pocket to check out later, I place the pictures the box and close the top, fighting with myself over whether to take it or not before giving in with a sigh.

Carrying it under my arm, I exit the storage

unit and head toward my car, pulling out my phone on the way. Once inside, I call the only person I'm acquainted with who might be able to help gather some information: Isaac.

A part of me expects he'll tell me the number leads to my father's accusation being true while the rest of me pretends finding out he'd been mistaken won't make a difference.

But the truth is, it will, and turns out waiting to know one way or the other is the hardest part.

"ARE YOU POSITIVE?"

"Yes." Isaac's sigh of frustration comes across clearly over the phone in response to my skepticism, a week after initially asking him to dig into the details. "Your father and Ivan Dorokhov were in business together. Damned hard to get specifics of what they were involved in after this long; anyone who might know anything won't speak about it. However, the investigator I hired assured me the same man who gave your father the identification documents received payment from Dorokhov for those services."

Dropping into my office chair, I stare at my computer screen while Joy walks into the room and shuts the door. "Fucking hell, this makes no sense."

"I agree. Everything my man found points

toward Dorokhov assisting your family, not attempting to murder you, which means you need to watch your fucking back. Somewhere in this chain of events, your father was lied to, and cut himself off from the only man who did everything he could to keep your family safe."

"How the hell did everything get fucked up? My father had to have known the documents came from Dorokhov. His daughter knew where to find me."

"No, she did not. Until she decided to take her trip, apparently the family only knew your identities, but not your location until they hired a P.I."

"So they could've found us anytime, but didn't? What the hell?"

"That is a question you will have to ask him yourself, Chandler, but if you decide to head to Russia, take my advice to watch your fucking back seriously. Somebody wanted your entire family dead, and are now aware of your continued existence if not your location."

Which they could damn well find with a little investigation, a fact which makes my confusion mount more by the second. "Goddammit. You know I have to go there now. Who knows if Ramona coming here has put her in danger the same as it has me."

"Yes, I figured you would." He clears his throat as if he wants to say something and after a moment continues with what sounds like…pity? "There is something else you might wish to know before you head that way."

Joy stares at me wide-eyed at my low growl and the irritation mixing with worry makes me snap at him. "Well, what the hell is it?"

"You've got two weeks until the wedding."

I don't have to ask whose wedding he refers to. Ramona had made it clear she would've been married long ago if not for the agreement and it makes sense her father would marry her off upon returning home without a groom. Not even the speed surprises me.

"Who?"

No need to elaborate as he replies, "Maksim Aristov. A well-educated, long-time friend of Miss Dorokhova, and poised to take over the family business when her father retires."

Ah. The man she spoke to in her apartment the night her cover blew up. "Are the nuptials a requirement for acquiring the business?"

"I am going to say no. As I understand from the information provided, Aristov takes over the family business whether or not he marries her. She will be provided for in either scenario."

Which begs the question, is she marrying him of her own accord or bowing to her father's wishes? And, whatever the answer to that question, do I have the right to go over there and potentially confuse her, even if it's only to make sure she's safe from an as yet unknown harm?

All these questions and hopefully soon I will have all the answers.

"Thanks for the assistance, Isaac. I'll let you know if I need anything else."

Hanging up the phone, Joy lifts an expectant brow and places her hands flat on the desk while studying me. "So?"

I can tell by the look in her eyes that she knows what will happen, but she wants to hear me say it.

"Looks like I'll need some bags packed for a trip to Russia."

She beams at me, not needing to respond before exiting the room to make sure I'm ready for the trip, leaving me alone with my thoughts and worries.

All of which are brought to life when I walk out of the Aeroport Pulkovo into the achingly cold evening air and two men flank me, one pressing the barrel of a gun into my left side with a menacing smirk as he speaks in heavily accented English.

"Mister Dorokhov has been expecting you."

AFFECTION

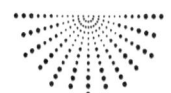

PART I
WITH THIS RING

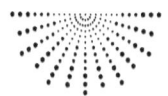

1

RAMONA

EACH TIME my father has a gathering or party, depending on the occasion, the first thing I wish for is an easy escape route for the moment all the socializing exhausts me.

However, there will be no escaping this evening.

Our wedding is two weeks away and tonight is the engagement dinner. Maksim is glued to my side, his hand resting on the exposed skin of my lower back, and smiling at every person in the room like the truly happy man he is.

I don't begrudge him his happiness because there's no question he loves me, but I do wish our feelings about each other were equal or, at least, closer than they are currently.

My emotions certainly haven't caught up with the change from friends to soon-to-be spouses. Tossed in with the current and future physical aspects, every inch of me is confused.

He hasn't pushed me to do anything sexual. In fact, he's seemed pleased since our first kiss just to be able to put his lips on me whenever we're together, and hasn't tried to go further. A good man to take his time and wait for me to be ready and any women would be glad to have someone like Maksim care about how his future wife feels.

Not that he knows about how far things went with O. Neither he nor my Papa would understand what happened between us, including the way O held me captive, even if it were only for a few days. And they most certainly wouldn't understand how I'm not angry about it or had sex with him after the fact.

With each day that passes, thinking about him happens less and less, and my pain at his rejection is slowly fading too. Plus, after two long weeks, if he thought he made a mistake he would've come here to find me already.

He's not chasing after me, and that means me not pursuing stupid romantic dreams and instead facing reality completely is a good idea.

"*Lyubimaya.*" Whispering 'sweetheart' in my ear, Maksim places his arm around my waist and squeezes affectionately to get my attention. "Thinking of how to escape the party, as you always do?"

Blinking, I realize we've actually been left alone for now, and turn my head to meet his amused gaze with a light snicker of my own. "You know me well. And you like to escape whenever possible as well."

His lips curve in remembrance of all the times we've slipped away and puts his empty champagne glass on a tray sitting on a nearby table.

Then, he moves his arms from my waist to grab my hand instead, interlacing our fingers together with a wink. "Come. I have something for you."

He leads us out of the room and down the hall, before taking the steps up to the bedrooms and stopping in front of the door to mine.

Keeping a grip on my one hand, he places his free one on the doorknob and chuckles. "Twenty years we have known each other and now I will see where you sleep for the first time."

Might be strange to some, but Papa made it clear when I was young that no boys were allowed to enter my room, not even my male friends. His excitement over something so small as this makes me giggle a little. "Hope you're not expecting anything too exciting."

He laughs as well, shakes his head, and turns the knob. Swinging the door open, he lets go of my hand and steps inside, only to turn around and shut it after I've entered.

"It is nice," he says with a whistle while walking closer to the center. "And not at all how I thought your room might be."

Glancing around the room at the cream

colored walls, dark green carpet, and trying not to draw his eyes to my bed, I point to the wall near us. "Yes, well, I grew out of pink wallpaper fifteen years ago, and begged mama and papa to redecorate."

"Ah yes." He snaps his fingers and grins. "I remember that story."

He leans back against the door and glances over at the bed, only returning his gaze back to me when I clear my throat and ask, "What do you have for me?"

Walking toward me, he reaches into his pocket and withdraws something from it at the exact moment he stops with our bodies nearly touching, his stance effectively keeping me up against the door.

Reaching up to cup my cheek, he caresses it lightly with the pad of his thumb and leans in to kiss my lips before drawing back enough to say, "I bought you a gift. Something from me to wear all the time."

He holds up a sparkling silver choker with a teardrop amethyst pendant dangling from it and indicates he wants me to turn around with his finger. There isn't much room between me and the door, but manage to do as he asks while biting my lip to remind him of my general dislike for jewelry.

It doesn't help that the moment the choker encircles my neck I'm reminded of the collar O had me wearing, and my eyes slam shut as Maksim takes his time fastening it in place before gently turning me back around to face him.

The choker's snugness and weight around my throat makes every swallow noticeable, and even though I won't say anything to him about it, the first thing I'll be doing once alone is taking it off. However, not wanting to hurt him for being thoughtful, I only smile and say, "Thank you."

"My pleasure, *malyshka*." Bringing his body flush with mine, his eyes blaze with interest as he traps me against the door and grabs my arms with his hands. "Place your hands flat against the door and don't move them."

He lets go without waiting for a response, and even as I flatten my hands against the door behind me as he demanded, the feel of his arousal against the front of my body surprises me. "What—?"

He places a finger against my lips to silence me and shakes his head, then drops both his hands to my sides to gather my skirt in his firm grasp. "No sex, I promise, but tonight I wish to please you. You will let me, won't you?"

Closing my eyes and whimpering at the sensuous glide of his right hand on the bare skin of my thigh, he uses the other to keep my skirt out of the way. Not waiting for a reply, he crushes my lips beneath his own and shoves aside the scrap of lace to touch me intimately between my legs with two fingers.

Although his movements are gentle, the hand between my leg is hot and rough. He forces my lips open with a thrust of his tongue and there's no stopping the jerk of my hips when he inserts one finger inside me, my sharp cry lost between our connected mouths.

Dragging his mouth away slowly, he sucks my tongue into his mouth before letting go and pushing another digit inside me with a raspy command. "Spread your legs a little for me, *lyubimaya.*"

He follows the order up with a quick withdrawal and deep stroke of his fingers, a third finger joining in the play, teasing and circling my clit as my wetness increases. And when all the sensations and my feelings collide, a sharp sob falls from my lips from enjoying it and hating the fact that I do.

Maksim's hands leave me, making my eyes pop open to find out what he's going to do next, and he smirks at me before sinking to his knees. Tugging my panties down my legs, he makes me step out of them along with my heels, and hikes my right leg over his shoulder as his head disappears under my skirt.

"Oh, Maksim, please——"

The feel of his mouth on me cuts off my protest, and his hands cup my ass to support my body after he puts my other leg over his shoulder as well. Licking my clit, while delving into my body with his tongue and fingers and using his mouth to mimic vibrations, his attention leaves me breathless. The pleasure I want and don't want all at the same time has me wishing for something to hold onto, especially when my body tightens only for it to release, dissolving into shockwaves that pulse through me.

Stopping the tears is impossible then. Bringing my hands up to cover my face, I weep into my hands while he lowers my feet to the ground and stands up.

Then, gathering me into his arms, he holds me snugly and tilts my chin up to gaze into my watery eyes with a sweet and understanding smile. "*Ty takaya krasivaya.*"

I don't feel so beautiful at this moment as tears trickle down my cheeks, but he's not expecting a response for his compliment as he lifts me in his arms and carries me toward the bed.

Setting me on my feet next to it, he unzips the back of my dress, presses a kiss to the nape of my neck just below the choker, and steps back. "Sleep well, *malyshka*. I will see you in the morning."

Unable to stop crying as he leaves the room and shut the door behind him, I strip the dress off and reach for the black silk robe laying over the back of my vanity chair. Slipping into it, I tie the belt around my waist and sit down in the chair, pulling out a make-up remover cloth and wiping at the mascara running down my face.

Tossing it in the small trash can next to the vanity, I lean in toward the mirror and examine the choker around my neck. It's more gorgeous than the glimpse I had of it earlier told me at roughly one-inch high, thin, and lined top to bottom as well as all around with…diamonds?

Getting as close to the mirror as I can, my eyes prick with renewed tears at realizing they are diamonds.

How the hell had Maksim afforded to buy such jewelry for me? The better question is why would he purchase something like this for me? I don't want it and tomorrow, I will tell him to take it back because it's too expensive even if we're going to marry. There are better things to spend money on than this.

However, after a quick stroke of the beautiful amethyst pendant dangling in front, my tears are quickly replaced by displeasure when I can't find the clasp to remove it. When my attempt to turn it around my neck fails from how close-fitting the choker hugs my throat, I head out of my room and down the hall toward the one he's staying in this evening thanks to the party.

Music and laughter drift upstairs to tell me the party's still going on, which means if I yell nobody is going to hear me, and that's what I plan to do as I knock angrily on his door. After a few moments where I have to wonder if he's going to answer because it's too loud for me to hear inside his room, he opens the door and grins as if he doesn't see me glaring at him.

"Miss me already, *lyubimaya*?"

Pointing at my neck, I storm inside his room and whirl around as he shuts the door, crossing my arms over my chest. "Remove the choker, Maksim. Now."

He frowns and mimics my stance with a shake of his head. "That's not going to happen."

"No? If you don't take it off, then I will find a way to do it myself."

With a hearty laugh, he strides to stand in front of me but is smart enough to keep his hands to himself with me angry as I am. "You will have a hard time finding someone willing to cut stainless steel so near to your neck."

Stainless steel and diamonds? No wonder it feels so heavy and restrictive.

"Please," I beg him with renewed tears. "Take it off. I won't be able to sleep with it on."

Lifting a hand to my face, he wipes at the wetness on my cheeks with a soft caress of his thumb, sighing as he shakes his head again. "No. It won't disturb your sleep. You will wear it because it marks you as mine, and it's beautiful on you. Don't ask me to remove it again."

Tears continue to trickle down my face as he slides his hand to my neck, caressing the choker while studying my face, and his tone changing to that of a man who knows how to get what he wants. "Soon you will be my wife. There has been no reason to wait to fuck you and kindness was the only reason I gave you time. I see now that was a wrong decision."

"It wasn't." Swiping at my face, I shake my head and try to step back, only for him to tighten his hold on my neck enough that escape is impossible. "I thought I could do this, Maksim, but I can't."

"You don't have a choice; why don't you understand that? You have a duty and you will fulfill it. We both will."

"What happened to me turning you down if I wish?"

"Doing something of your own accord will always remain preferable to being forced, don't you agree?" Although the look in his eyes softens, there's no sign of remorse in his gaze for the subtle threat, and he doesn't loosen his grip as he continues in a gentle, firm tone. "You'll stop waiting for him, *malyshka*. I told you he wouldn't give you what you sought and I was right. He isn't coming to save you."

Just because I know it's true doesn't mean his words cut any less and the pain in my chest intensifies. "No need for you to be cruel—"

He cuts me off with a punishing kiss, bringing his other hand up to the belt at my waist to loosen it, and slips his hand into the robe when it gapes open. Pushing it off my shoulders, the fabric drops to the floor with ease as he skims his fingers along the soft skin of my stomach. Flattening out once his hand is close my side, he slips his arm around my waist and jerks my body almost violently toward his until we're flush against each other.

He continues ravishing my mouth with one hand around my neck, walking forward until the bed bumps against the back of my legs, and then abruptly releases me. However, he doesn't let me fall back to land on it. Instead, he grabs my falling body and whirls me around, shoving me so I'm bent over at the waist with my face down on the blanket.

Invading my body with two of his fingers, they are savage even though he's trying to be gentle because he doesn't want to hurt me. He's bound by duty as much as I am and not following through on those obligations comes with consequences neither of us wishes to experience.

He leans over my body while fingering me, showering kissed on my jaw before whispering in my ear, "You're so wet for me, *malyshka*. I told you we would be good together, didn't I?"

Then, the fingers are gone and I feel the tip of his cock at the entrance to my body. Slamming my eyes shut, I wonder what Maksim would think if he knew the only man I'm wet for, as he thrusts inside me with a contented groan, is the man everyone wants me to forget.

2

OWEN

CONFISCATING MY PHONE AND BELONGINGS, the two men shove me into the car after searching me for hidden weapons and one stays with me in the back with a gun pointed in my direction while the other drives the car.

He wouldn't shoot me even if I tried to escape because Dorokhov would hardly want me to be dead on arrival. However, they do surprise me by pulling up to a dingy-looking warehouse Dorokhov must use instead of his house, and the man in the back who hasn't spoken a word all evening keeps his gun aimed at me while leading me inside.

The setup is nicer than I expected to see upon entering, with stairs that lead to a second floor lined with doors — probably to offices or storage rooms — and rows of shelves filled with boxes filling up half the floor.

Dorokhov is speaking with a man similar in looks to the other two and I admire the fact he isn't taking any chances, especially when the two who brought me here guard the front doors after advising me where to stand while waiting.

Upon catching sight of our entry, he dismisses the other man with a wave as he walks this way, stopping to stand within a foot of me with a smile that doesn't fool me on his face as he speaks in Russian.

"Thank you for coming, Odin."

My response is in English, already annoyed by his deliberate baiting, along with his robust and healthy appearance. "The name's Owen Chandler."

He switches to English with a smirk. "I know your name, boy. Your father and I were friends long before your birth." Then, without warning, his fist connects with my stomach, causing me to bend over and cough. While I attempt to catch my breath, he pulls up a chair and forces me to sit on it. "That was for locking up my daughter and sleeping with her, *vy ublyudok*."

I may be a motherfucker, but how the hell…? He insults me again when I lift my head with my brows raised in curiosity.

"*Glupyy*." Stupid. "You think me a fool who would send my daughter without someone to keep an eye on her? You released her before those who watched her for me could get inside and rip you apart."

Many things to say, none of them wise, and definitely nothing he wants to hear. "Your daughter was well cared for in the brief time she spent at my home."

"*Net*. You took advantage of and hurt her. Cared for? *Da*, since returning home she is."

Feeling guilty enough as it is, I nod at him and straighten in my seat as the pain in my stomach begins to subside. "Look, I didn't come here to discuss my relationship with your daughter. I need some answers."

His lips curl in a half-snarl. "There is no relationship between you and my daughter."

Shoving a hand through my hair, I blow out a breath and change the topic. "Tell me about my father and how you knew I would make my way here."

"People are predictable, including you. Anyone sticking their nose in my business for answers gets back to me around here." He doesn't sit, standing in front of me with his arms crossed and a scowl on his face, the look he directs me reminding me of my father when I was a child. "As for your father, I understand he kept you ignorant of relevant facts and will answer any questions you have."

"Did you set the fire?"

His countenance expresses how crazy he thinks that question is and tells me Ramona hadn't mentioned it to him, which begs the question why hadn't she? "The fire was your father's idea."

"What?" Jumping up from my chair, I quickly sit back down when the guards aim their guns at me. "I nearly became trapped in that fire; my father wouldn't have done that to his own family."

"You weren't supposed to be out of bed. It was a controlled fire, meant to make it look as though someone wanted your family dead even though everyone escaped safely, and you getting out of bed fucked up the plan."

Remembering my father scolding me for not being in my bed, I shake my head at how scared he must've been and ask the most important question I have now. "Why risk it?"

"When your father picked teaching as his profession to start over in America with, I thought him a fool. A man like your father, one of the biggest arms dealers in Russia, teaching at a college for the rest of his life?" My face exhibits the astonishment I feel at this news and he laughs heartily. "Wanted out of the business and a fresh start. He wouldn't be talked out of it and made plans to live in America with new identities. You will always be Owen Chandler now, but only because everyone was told Odin and his parents died on their way to America."

I hear everything he says even as my brain latches on to the new information about my father. Arms dealer? This information changes everything known about my parents. Shoving a hand through my hair, I stare at him before deciding to tell him what I've thought all this time. "He told me it was you."

He laughs heartily as if that's the funniest thing he's ever heard, and maybe it is. "Of course, he would say such a thing as he never intended to return to Russia. He didn't want you to find out about his life here and have your memories ruined by the truth."

Fuck, I feel as if the joke is on me here…"Then why send your daughter to America? Why talk to her about us marrying all these years, something my own father never spoke of?"

"Such an agreement never existed." He shrugs with an unrepentant expression even for all his lies. "She was so young when you two met, yet she remembered you, and asked about your family every year. Just a young girl who heard your mother joke about you two marrying and never let it go."

Confirmation of the memory I had being real doesn't ease the sick feeling in the pit of my stomach knowing all the information he's hiding from Ramona. "So you lied to your daughter? For what? To keep her from marrying anyone except a man of your choice?"

"An astute observation. A good thing she never caught on to my plans for Maksim to marry her once he had matured enough to lead the business and build a good life for them."

This is unbelievable, and my fists curl with the urge to punch him for treating his daughter as nothing more than property. "Holy fucking shit, have you ever been honest a day in your life?"

His eyes flash, his whole body tensing before he relaxes with a chuckle, and directs a pointed stare at me. "Now you know why you were punched. America was nothing more than a distraction to set things in motion here at home; never thought she would fail to see you for the asshole you are or that you would fuck her. But she's a good girl and will do what she's told."

"Goddamn. I'm not a father, but how could you do this to her? Is she nothing more than a chess piece to you? A pawn in a power game?"

"What I do with my daughter is none of your business." He snaps his fingers, and the two men from the car are at my side in seconds, each grabbing an arm so I can't escape. "And to make sure you don't try to stop the wedding or something equally stupid such as reckless bravery, it's your turn to be held against your will. You will be escorted to the airport once you are no longer able to interfere."

He nods at the men. "You have your orders." Then, as they lead me toward the steps leading up to the offices, he calls out in Russian. "Viktor, bring me his things after he's taken care of. I need to keep his assistant from getting suspicious."

Fuck. Joy's intelligent enough to notice if something's amiss, but if he gets a feel for what to say, she won't realize she's being duped. I'm pissed at myself for coming here without protection; this is what I get for trying to believe someone outside my small circle of friends is honorable.

Idiot. And how big of an idiot is evident when, once we've read the top of the steps, the silent driver named Viktor and the other man place me in a mostly dark room in the corner. The room isn't much; practically empty with nothing more than a cot in one corner and a urinal in the other, and definitely no way to escape.

After shoving me inside, Viktor leaves, and the other man points the gun at me while laughing at me staring at the window.

"Can't see in, and nobody can hear any noise you make, in case you were thinking of trying something funny. Enjoy the show," he grunts before pulling the door shut, the click of a lock following in an instant.

Standing close to the one-way window, I smack it only to instantly regret doing so, because the lack of noise makes it as if I never hit it and now my hand hurts for fucking nothing. A mystery as to how they managed to arrange the room this way.

Watching Viktor hand my phone to Dorokhov, who then scrolls through for a moment before looking toward the room I'm in with a smile, makes me hope that one day I can get my hands around his fucking neck to wring it.

For now, I flip him off for my own sake before turning toward the cot, trying to figure out what I can do to get out of here if anything.

I hadn't watched my back, and when Isaac hears of this once I'm free, the chance of him letting me forget it are zilch.

But hey, the one thing I'm grateful for as I sit down is that they let me remain clothed.

WHILE TRAPPED IN THE ROOM, NOTHING IS GIVEN to me except a few basics. My clothes from my luggage; a cheap paper bowl with water, bar of soap, and a rag they say is to wash with, and food delivered three times a day — gun in Viktor's hand as he opens the door and sets it on the floor.

My view, however, gives me an impressive sight of the front interior of the building, as well as all the product coming in and out of it. The information something I file away for later even if it's useless to anyone except me; the police here are getting their hands greased to ignore an operation like this one.

Between that occasionally and sleep, I spend every other waking moment thinking about how my father lied about his life and the fire, leaving me to wonder if anything he ever told me was the truth. And the same for my mother.

Ruined my memories? Absolutely, but despite my feelings upon arriving here, my extreme relief is the one I'm focusing on. Nobody tried to kill my family.

No one is going to come after Ramona for knowing the 'truth' because the truth has been known all along to those involved in it. A fire, new identities, and fake deaths, all orchestrated by two lifelong friends.

I don't think anybody could have made this shit up better.

And I'm trapped here. There's no way out. Too many people around all day, and I've spent quite a few hours each night trying to find a way out, but like their plan to help my father start a new life, this room is just as well orchestrated.

However, instead of feeling sorry for myself, I focus all my thoughts on Ramona, hoping she's strong enough to survive the life her father is about to involve her in if she's clueless. No, there's no way she knows about it, about what actually goes on and it leaves me wishing I could protect her, save her.

It's a foolish hope since I can't even save my fucking self and she deserves better.

AS HER WEDDING DAY CREEPS CLOSER, SO DOES MY freedom, and I keep track of the days in my head, thinking of all the ways to help Ramona once I can go home to involve others, such as Isaac if he doesn't act like a total dick, in the plan.

I start to think I'll never catch a glimpse of her before the wedding, but then with two days left before the nuptials, Maksim walks inside the warehouse with Ramona at his side.

She looks beautiful with her hair hanging down her back, but the rest of her is covered up by a dark coat, her face free of the make-up she wore when we met.

Dorokhov greets her with a kiss on the cheek and his future son-in-law with a pat on the back before turning to indicate the rest of the warehouse with an outward sweep of his arm. From this distance, it's hard to see her expressions, but she walks beside Maksim while her father leads them around the bottom floor, her back straight and looking forward at all times with her arm looped through his.

As they head up the steps my heart pounds, even knowing she won't be able to see me doesn't keep me from waiting for them to walk past the room.

Her father keeps talking as they walk and as they start to pass by my room, Ramona stops in front of the mirror and turns to look at it, but Maksim grabs her chin in a punishing-looking grip and forces her to meet his gaze instead.

Unable to read his lips to see what he's saying, I squelch the desire to punch him for handling her that way, and even though she squares her shoulders and nods, the sight of her lower lip trembling shows her lack of confidence in whatever they're discussing.

When his hand lowers to her neck, my eyes widen enough to hurt at the sight of what looks like a tight-fitting diamond choker around her throat. The possessive placement of his hand along with the crowding of her personal space, towering over her to intimidate, all point to the decoration serving as a collar to declare her as his.

Stroking his thumb over it, she closes her eyes, the growing blush on her cheeks telling me she's embarrassed to have him acknowledge it — which confirms my suspicions — and then he leans in to say something against her lips before kissing her.

A quick glance at Dorokhov declares his amusement at this little display right in front of the window where I'll see it, and with a few words — probably asking them to if they are ready to continue — Maksim steps back from Ramona following another few words.

I watch as she loops her arm back through his, lowers her gaze to stare at the floor, and swipes at a tear sliding down her cheek as they start walking again.

This is the confirmation I need to verify that Ramona needs saving as much as I do; I just hope by the time I can help her it isn't too late.

3

RAMONA

On the morning of our wedding, Maksim covering my naked form with his own wakes me up. He buries his face in my shoulder as I wrap my legs around him in the way he told me he prefers, and his hand presses against my mouth to stifle the whimpers and moans evoked by the hard thrusts of his dick that affect me even though I don't want them to.

He kisses my neck and shoulder before going lower, biting and sucking my nipples and the soft skin around them, leaving behind marks I'll see when dressing for the day. Now that my father's given him permission to stay here until the wedding, every morning is like this; he doesn't require my participation beyond the minimum he demands.

Today, though, his thrusts are measured, with him pulling all the way to the edge before slamming back in, and I get the feeling he's still punishing me for getting upset at the warehouse the other day.

After spending all day preparing for the wedding, I had wanted to go home, but Maksim insisted on showing me one of my father's warehouses. I have never been in one before, so I thought it would be interesting, but after twenty minutes I asked if we could leave.

Maksim's display of authority to put me in 'my place' in front of my father had embarrassed me, but he only seems to care if my complaining humiliates him. Apparently before our engagement, I had the freedom to say whatever I wanted, but now I'm not to speak unless the words coming out of my mouth are positive.

He says it's for my own protection, but since he won't tell me what or who I need protecting from, I don't believe him.

Pulling out once he's forced my body to orgasm, he lifts his body off mine a little, the silent signal for me to turn on my stomach, and rest on my knees with me face down on the pillow.

"You'll be good today, *malyshka*." He grabs my hair in his fist when I'm in the desired position and wraps it around his hand, pulling my head back until tears prick my eyes from the pain. "And to make sure you'll behave and do what must be done, I'm going to give you something else to think about all day."

No way out with him holding onto my hair as

he is, and I sob at the feel of him hard and prodding my ass, where's he's been prepping me — as he called it — with his fingers for days now.

"Breathe, *lyubimaya*, and do what I've taught you," he says in a firm, aroused tone. "How easy this is is up to you."

Sobbing, I clutch the sheets in my fists, the pain unbearable while pushing back against him, following his instructions just like a dutiful wife would. It is the title I'll officially have in a few short hours, after all.

However, 'easy' is never how I will refer to my giving in to his commands; this is simply a situation where he has all the power and we both know it.

And I was wrong; Maksim will hurt me if it means keeping me in line and reminding me who's in charge every chance he gets.

~

AS A YOUNG GIRL, I HAD MANY DREAMS OF WHAT my wedding would be like when it came time to marry the man I would spend the rest of my life with.

The reality is harsh and unforgiving. My reflection stares back at me, unsmiling, from the full-length mirror in front of me. With my hair curled and lips painted, the ivory wedding gown with its long lacy sleeves and sweetheart neckline adorns and clings to my body, an amethyst colored sash added last moment to match the pendant on my choker at Maksim's insistence. My mama smiles in pride from where she stands beside me.

"You are beautiful." She steps close to kisses my cheek, her brown eyes watering as her face grows solemn. "My only child becoming a wife to a wonderful man today, and someday soon, you'll become a mother to your own children. That is my hope for you."

Her comment worries me; not due to her looking forward to becoming a *babushka*, but because having children in the future hasn't even crossed my mind. I don't know about Maksim, but since he's been having unprotected sex with me, her wish to be a babushka may happen sooner rather than later.

If he hasn't gotten me pregnant, I'll have to talk to him when my period arrives as it's due any day now, and ask if we can wait on having children. Framing it as us having more time alone together should work best, but the truth is I'm not ready to parent a child yet and am even less sure of sharing that duty with him.

Adjusting to the rougher, firmer version of Maksim as well as marriage to him is enough to handle for the time being.

Thankfully, there is just the civil ceremony at ZAGS and a small dinner for our families today. No official celebration that might last for a week, which I am grateful for, because genuine happiness about this marriage isn't something I'll be able to fake convincingly. Maksim made everyone laugh with his 'oops, booked honeymoon on the wrong date' to explain why the wedding festivities will be cut short, but my gut instinct suspects it was deliberate.

Spending a month-long honeymoon to a 'surprise location,' away from family and familiar surroundings, and all alone with my new husband doesn't sound good either.

My mama's eyes are still on mine through the mirror, and for a second, the urge to confide in her and tell her about my time in the USA takes over, words on the tip of my tongue tripping over themselves while trying to spill out.

But her gaze breaks with mine as the door opens, and she turns her smile at Maksim when he steps into the room, walking over to greet him with a kiss on each cheek. Then, she ruins my chances to make a decision with him about children later with her innocent, excited and completely justified considering the occasion comment.

"We were just talking about what beautiful children you two will have, perhaps some day soon. You will make me a proud *babushka*, no?"

Maksim's delighted smile matches the pleasure in his eyes, staring at me as he takes her hands in his and kisses the tops of them before promising her, "You won't have to wait long for *vnuchata*. Having a house full of children with my love will bring me much joy."

"Of course."

He releases her hands with a nod and walks over to stand behind me, examining me in the mirror before squeezing my shoulders in approval and turning me to face him. Keeping my eyes lowered in deference, he presses up on my chin so I know he wants me to raise my gaze and says to my mother, "We will be down in a few."

Her cue to leave disguised as a statement, something she takes in stride because she's used to it from my father, and the sound of the door closing makes my stomach clench.

"Your sweet cooperation pleases me, *lyubimaya*." His hands move to span my waist, his mouth finding my neck as he kisses the sensitive flesh just below the choker, and skims his lips up until they are next to my ear while one hand moves to rest flat on my stomach. "The image of you carrying my child is an enjoyable one. Perhaps you already are, hm?"

"It's possible," I whisper in reply because he expects one, but every part of me hopes not yet. And maybe never.

"Good." Straightening, he pecks my lips before making my heart drop into my stomach as he says, "I have something for you."

He lowers his body, crouching in front of me

even while making sure my gaze stays locked with his, and his hands under my dress.

Running his hands up both my legs, he cups an ass cheek in each hand and squeezes them, smirking at me when I whimper softly. "Tender?"

"A little."

Gliding his hands back down my legs, he chuckles softly and lets my skirt drop before rising, directing me to turn around with a circular motion of one finger. "Face the mirror, bend over and spread that gorgeous ass of yours for me. No tears, *malyshka*; there's no time to fix your makeup if you ruin it."

My skirts are lifted and tossed over my head a few second later, his hands caressing and stroking my legs before squeezing the cheeks as I hold them, and licks my pussy with a long, slow stroke of his tongue.

He's mastered my body at this point, knowing how and where to touch with his fingers and lick with his tongue to get a response, and even as he brings me closer to orgasm my mind waits for the 'something' he has for me.

He sucks my clit into his mouth and nips it with his teeth, sending me hurtling over the edge with a small cry of pleasure, but I know better than to move even as my legs threaten to collapse beneath me.

Then he pushes something cold and hard against the hole where he left me aching this morning, securing me in his hold with an arm around my waist with me still bent over while shoving the object past my body's natural resistance.

I don't cry at the feeling of fullness, similar to how it felt earlier having him inside of me, but I definitely despise it. My eyes grow watery as tears threaten to overflow, but squeezing my eyes shut prevents any from falling as he grabs my arms and slowly pulls up until I'm standing straight and facing him again.

"Pity we need to leave now, *lyubimaya*, as I want nothing more than to fuck you with that plug lodged deep in your ass."

Sniffling, I lower my gaze at the smug and desirous expression on his face as I whisper, "Why do you do these things to me?"

"Because I like it, and in time, you will want it as much as I do and beg me for it."

At that he takes my hand and leads me out of the room, every step reminds me what he's done and will continue to do to me. The car ride to ZAGS is spent biting my lip, my whole body rigid in the attempt to keep from being jostled while Maksim watches me the whole trip with barely concealed glee.

It's a look he continues to wear throughout the ceremony, gazing into my eyes while slipping his ring on my hand, all the while I silently wish O would burst through the door. A hope that follows me when we're pronounced husband and wife, through the breaking of the crystal glasses, and the whole ride back to my parent's house instead of doing the traditional traveling around the city.

Sending me upstairs to change into a different dress for dinner — one he chose for me to wear tonight when we leave on our trip — Maksim slips his hand under the table to cup me between my legs after I return downstairs and take the seat to his left at the dinner table.

Through the toasts, the drinks, the kissing, and the food, my gaze occasionally flicks toward the door in a hope that's dying a slow, painful death, until finally Maksim pinches my thigh hard and leans toward me to hiss in my ear as I bite back a gasp of pain. "Keep your eyes on your plate unless you're being spoken to. If you look at the door one more time, you won't like the consequences."

I already don't, but do as he says, and the roughest emotional moment arrives when it's time for us to leave on our trip.

The bags are in the limo, Maksim stands by the car door watching me where I stand on the top step, my mother hugging me tight before turning to head inside after a final kiss goodbye. My father, however, doesn't hug me; he's never been the affectionate type.

Instead, he stands with his hands behind his back and says, "Enjoy your trip, *kotenok*."

I try to smile at his good wishes but fail, only

able to manage to keep from full-out frowning. "Thank you, Papa."

He steps closer then, putting his hand on my shoulder, and clasping it tight before letting go just as quickly. "I know it is an adjustment, and in time, everything will become easier. Your behavior so far has made me proud, *kotenok*. Do not disappoint me now."

His praise means so much, it's hard to swallow past my anger at myself for not fighting harder before it got this far, but it's too late now. "I won't."

Nodding, he goes inside and shuts the door without another word or backward glance, and the last tendril of my hope that someone will put a stop to this day finally dies.

I give in to the inevitable with dry, downcast eyes, and a coldness takes over my heart before spreading through every limb in a way I'm not sure will ever thaw.

4

OWEN

"GET UP." Dmitry — my time here has taught me the name of Viktor's partner — stands inside the door holding out a plate of food, and waits patiently for me to get out of bed to grab it from him.

As I sit back down and begin to eat, Dorokhov replaces Dmitry's position in the doorway, and he doesn't have to say a word as he stares at me with a cocky smile.

Ramona was married off to Maksim yesterday and both are out of my reach...for now.

"Thank you for your cooperation in this matter, Mister Chandler. Once you've finished with your breakfast, Viktor will escort you to the airport and assist you to make sure you head home safely."

Seething at his cordial tone — as if he hadn't kept me locked up in here for two weeks — the desire to punch him in his face is hard to ignore, but I won't do it. Not worth the effort, or the beatdown I'll receive in reciprocation.

When I don't reply with more than a curt nod, he turns to leave, only to turn back around and pinning me with a hard stare. "I trust you won't sniff around my daughter in the future, Mister Chandler. There isn't a power strong enough in the world to help you get close to her now."

I grin at the not so subtle threat and stand after sitting the empty plate on the floor. "Why the need to warn me to stay away then?"

His lips curl, his gaze is contemptuous. "I may be in business with criminals, but murder is below me. Those closest to me, however, won't hesitate to take care of the problem if you try to take what is theirs."

Add Maksim to the list of people I need to gather information about before coming back here. "Duly noted."

My response coupled with a mock salute is ripe with sarcasm and after a moment, the smug smile returns as he exits the room with a shrug. He's done with me, and he might have won for now.

And his mistake in letting me go will come back to bite him. For now, I'll go home and bide my time, formulate the perfect plan to free Ramona.

She deserves a choice in the life she leads, even if in the end she doesn't choose me.

~

JOY, WHO'S WAITING FOR ME IN THE BAGGAGE claim area, runs into my arms with a cry of relief the moment she sees me.

Her hug lasts for mere seconds before she takes a step back and pinches her nose even as her fingers fondle the full-beard gracing my face. "You need a shower and a shave the moment we get home. I almost didn't recognize you."

Can't blame her for stepping away. I tried to wash off in the airport as best I could, but it wasn't enough. I probably need a whole bar of soap and a scrub brush. Either way, my brief enjoyment is teasing her by stroking the beard and grinning when she glares. "It itched at first, but I'm used to it now. You don't like it?"

"God no." She twists her lips and glances at the carousel when it beeps to let us know the luggage is coming. "You're lucky to have texted me when you did about coming back. He did a good job of tricking me at first, but you never go more than a day without talking to me so I knew something was wrong."

"Nothing you could've done except get yourself put in that room with me, Joy, so I'm glad you didn't manage to get that far. He's an asshole who wanted his daughter to do as he said and took measures to prevent any interference."

"The wedding took place?" At my nod, her

eyes water and she bites her lip, glancing away before looking back at me while squaring her shoulders. "I feel sorry for her. Did you, at least, learn about your father?"

"He isn't the man I thought he was."

The luggage conveyor moves behind us and as we wait for mine, I fill her in on what I've learned. By the time we're headed out to the car, she's shaking her head in disbelief much as I had.

"Owen, it can't be true. He's lied about so much, surely he's lying about your father as well."

"He isn't." Reaching the car, the driver opens the trunk and stick my bags in while Joy and I climb into the warm interior, tears streaming down her cheeks as I shut the door and explain. "Dorokhov had photographic and paper evidence he brought in to show me one day. All fake? Certainly can't put it past him, but it's a lot of effort to falsify that amount of proof. As Isaac said, damned hard to get the truth when nobody will speak up; their silence is bought and paid for."

When the car begins to move she finally speaks, her hand comes to rest on mine, and her voice soft and reassuring as usual. "Your father, no matter his life in Russia, got you away and was one of the best men I've ever met. This changes nothing about the life your father gave you here, except now you know nobody is after you."

"For now."

Her voice registers true alarm. "What?"

"Saving Ramona will certainly have her father, along with her husband and those who protect him, coming after me."

"Does she want you to save her, Owen? It is twenty-sixteen. She didn't have to go through with the wedding; she chose to."

"No, she didn't, Joy. Her father orchestrated it for many years and sent her on the trip here to prepare for it without her knowing. She's a good girl and does as she's told — his words, not mine."

"I see. But nothing is as we thought it was, so this is me taking back what I said before you left. You barely know her, you were never promised to her, and you have no obligation—"

"Joy." My interruption is soft and firm, her eyes going round at the frown on my face. "I do now. She is innocent and has no idea how much her father has betrayed and continues to abuse, her trust. No good man would ignore it, especially with knowing what I do. Not when I can potentially put a stop to it."

With shining eyes, she gives me a watery smile and nods. "Okay, but promise me you'll be careful, especially for her. We must make sure it's what she wants before doing anything; we don't have the right to ruin her life unless she wants our help."

Ruin Ramona's life? Far from it. "Absolutely. The last thing I wish to do is hurt her or put her in danger."

"I never thought I'd see this day."

"What day?"

She sits back, clasping her hands in her lap, a beautiful grin replacing the sadness filling her face moments before. "The day when you're willing to go through so much effort for a woman. Didn't get to spend much time with her, because you're an idiot who let her go when she didn't want to leave, but she got under your skin anyway."

When I merely stare at her, because there's no point in denying the truth, she giggles and says, "I thought so."

"Yes, well." Clearing my throat, I reach out and grab her wrist, pulling her toward me with little resistance until our faces are inches apart. "I liked her, but it may lead to nothing. She and Maksim were friends, and you're right, she may have married him willingly. Perhaps it was simply the speed at which she went from being with me to marrying him that made her look sad that day. She thought a lie true for decades, I had no idea, and so she was still coming to terms with reality."

She understands what I'm saying as I thought she would, lifting her hand to rest on my chest, adjusting to sitting on her knees to make her position more comfortable. "You don't want to get your hopes up and you shouldn't. It's better to remain pragmatic and a little detached until you know for sure."

"We were never together."

"You weren't, and you have needs Owen. I've

never known you to go without fulfilling them because you've made it clear they're like a beast you must feed. You aren't disloyal when you've never made any promises, but I can see how you might need someone to tell you that right now."

"Tell me why." I know why, but want to hear her say it; to have my feelings validated in a world that might tell me I'm wrong.

"Other than Simone, you've never liked someone to the point where you thought it might have a chance of going further. But not playing or sleeping with anyone while you wait to find out if she wants you or not doesn't lessen or negate how much you like her. You're not unfaithful because you've got nothing between you two to cheat on."

"You're right."

"Of course, I am. Life isn't a romance novel. You don't know her well enough to love her and remaining celibate to prove...what? That you're serious about pursuing her if you're given the chance? That is stupid and not real." She pulls back with a wrinkle of her nose, the action cute enough I let go of her wrist when she tugs on it and scoots away while changing the topic. "You really stink and that beard needs to go a.s.a.p. It really doesn't suit you."

Two things we've already established and her deflection makes me smile, watching her lips part and her skin flush as I level her with a knowing stare. "I'll take care of both those issues when we get home, Joy, and then you'll let me take care of you."

"W-what?"

Her blush deepens at my slow perusal of her. "I know what you need, and how long you've gone without it." I may consider her my family, but in the sense of how much we mean to one another, not in the traditional sense. She's an attractive woman in every way.

"Owen." She sucks in a breath, glancing out the window before bring her softened gaze back to mine, shining with emotion. "We haven't played in years. What makes you think we should now?"

"Trust. We both have needs and know where we stand with one another. No drama, no distractions…and while this is going on, that's exactly what I require."

Her tongue darts out to wet her lips, and anyone who didn't know Joy as well as I do might take her looking back out the window without speaking as a 'no,' especially when silence falls between us for a while.

But she crosses and uncrosses her legs, sighing each time, and as we turn onto the final street before reaching home, Joy turns back to me with her flip switched just as I knew she would.

Gone is my assistant and partner, and in her place, the submissive, playful part of my best friend shines from her needy eyes. "Okay."

"I won't go easy on you tonight."

Her lips curve in anticipation, matching the excitement in her eyes as the car turns into the driveway, her tongue darting out as she whispers, "Perfect. Easy is the last thing I want. I need to forget as much as you do right now."

One shower, shave, and warm-up later, the first sharp strike of the cane against Joy's bare ass is everything we both need and, for a little while, takes my mind off all the fucking things I can't change immediately.

5

RAMONA

"Welcome to beautiful Antigua, Mister and Missus Kozar. Thank you for choosing to spend your honeymoon here."

Both Maksim and I smile at the woman behind the desk, but he takes care of everything to do with the room while I say nothing as per his order.

I had no idea we weren't traveling under our real names until we were on the private plane and Maksim told me both he and my father thought it best for our privacy and safety. We were more likely to be left alone to enjoy our honeymoon if everyone thinks we're someone else. I suppose in a way it makes sense, but when has anyone ever cared about my connection to my own father?

Maybe it just matters more outside of Russia, so I took his word for it and try to remember to respond to the false name. After the close to sixteen-hour flight, that's easy to do since all I want to do is sleep; keeping my gaze lowered helps prevents people from trying to engage me in conversation.

"Come, *lyubimaya*."

Maksim grabs my elbow and leads me out of the main building, a man following behind us with our bags down the sidewalk through the humid air and darkening skies as nighttime nears, and stop in front of a building not far from the shoreline.

Unlocking the door, he swings it open and lets go of my arm, leaving me to head inside as he turns to tip the man once he sets our bags down. The interior of the suite is gorgeous. Open floor plan with white walls and furniture, a TV on one wall, full-kitchen, and French windows…all this is taken in by me with a single glance.

As Maksim shuts the door, I keep walking into the bedroom, finding a king-size bed, an en-suite bathroom, and balcony door. Returning to the living room to find him standing in front of the television flipping through the stations, he shuts it off with a dissatisfied grunt when I stop a few feet from him and points to the luggage.

"Put our things away and then get a shower."

Stepping forward with a nod, I grab the handles of the bags, only for him to pinch my chin hard between his thumb and two fingers as he frowns at me. "You will acknowledge me with a 'husband' in every statement, whether we are alone or in the company of others, and do as I say immediately. Disrespect nor defiance will be tolerated. Understand?"

Another thing to add to the list of stuff he requires of me, to remind me of my place, and his position as head of our house. "Yes, husband, I understand."

The hardness in his eyes melts, his whole countenance softening as his hand drops to my neck to stroke the choker with his thumb, and then he surprises me. "Turn around so I can remove this."

Hardly going to argue against being free of the choker for even a short while, I do as he says and sigh with relief when the weight is gone from my neck within seconds. Thanks to some angling with a hand mirror weeks ago, I know the enclosure requires a combination of four numbers to take off and have felt nothing except dread since searching the internet only to discover the solution is one of ten-thousand.

Figure it out on my own? Not fucking likely.

Appreciation for being able to breathe and swallow like normal for the first time in over a month, I face him again, this time with a genuine smile. "Thank you, husband."

Then, before he can change his mind, I take the handles of the luggage and roll them toward the room to do as he said. Naturally, I discover why he wanted me to put the clothes away first, because after emptying his luggage, I open mine to find everything from new lingerie to sundresses, as well as a peach colored bikini that won't leave much to the imagination.

Choosing a black babydoll with matching panties, I stash the now empty bags into the closet, and shut it before heading into the bathroom to shower while praying he won't put that choker back on me tonight.

HE'S WAITING FOR ME IN BED, SITTING ON TOP OF the blankets completely nude, when I walk out of the bathroom after drying my wet hair.

"Come here." He doesn't give me time to feel shy about all the skin showing in this little outfit, patting the space between his legs and directing me so I'm kneeling between his legs while facing him after I climb onto the bed. Fisting the base of his cock in one hand, he clutches my hair in the other. "I want to fuck that beautiful mouth of yours and then we can rest."

Trapped in his grasp, I open my mouth wide as he shoves my head down, and instantly gag when he thrusts into the back of my throat, holding my head immobile as he groans.

I try not to swallow because every time I do he grunts and pushes deeper even if there's nowhere for him to go, and begin sobbing when he picks up speed while maintaining his depth.

"Hands behind your back," he demands harshly when instinct has me pushing against his thighs to free myself and plunges harder when I clasp them together. "Ah, *malyshka*, your mouth is almost as good as fucking your ass."

I fear he'll decide to finish there instead with that comment, but after another deep thrust, he holds my head down on his cock even though I'm struggling to breathe, and makes sure I have no choice except to swallow as he comes.

Then, after yanking me up by my hair enough his cock slips free of my mouth, he keeps my head bent, bares my neck, and secures that fucking choker back around it.

"Sit up."

When I do my cheeks are wet with tears, and he wiggles one finger in front of my face before dropping it out of my sight, tugging harshly on something around my neck that makes my head move as if I'm nothing more than a rag doll.

"I saw the hope in your eyes, *zhena*." He keeps my head bent so I can't look at him, the word 'wife' on his lips filled with affection from me that I should feel but don't. "Hope that I wouldn't put this back on you. I took it off to switch the pendant with another more useful attachment, that is all. The way I fixed it makes them interchangeable without needing to remove it from your neck again."

Letting go, he tilts my chin up by pressing one

finger on it and he smirks since my gaze is lowered as always. "Not only will I control your body with this if I desire to, *malyshka*, it also tells me of your location at all times."

My stomach picks that moment to roll, perhaps heaving in rebellion at how inescapable this marriage, this restricted and monitored life with Maksim truly is, and when the feeling doesn't subside, I struggle against his hold with a distressed cry. "I'm going to be sick!"

Instantly releasing me with a concerned frown, I scramble off the bed and barely make it to the toilet, wailing while clutching the seat desperately. There's no feeling worse in the world than puking.

Or having someone witness it.

But as Maksim pulls my hair away from my face and rubs my back, suddenly that doesn't matter. He soothes me the best he can as my body revolts until there's nothing left, and after helping me freshen up, he comforts me just like a loving husband should as exhaustion draws me into a deep sleep while wrapped in his warm embrace.

THE NEXT MORNING, FOR THE FIRST TIME SINCE WE began having sex, I'm not woken up by Maksim climbing on top of me.

As it happens, he isn't in bed at all, and an unexplainable guilt takes over when a glance at the clock declares it ten a.m., which is pretty late for me as I'm normally up by seven. Wary of getting sick again, I sit up nice and slow before tossing back the covers and slipping out of bed.

Wandering into the bathroom to brush my teeth, the sight of my pale face and messy hair in the mirror makes me grimace and try to make myself more presentable before heading to look for Maksim.

The sound of his laughter greets me as I walk into the kitchen, and the smile on his face when he sees me is nothing compared to the shock on mine at seeing him cooking, nor when he points at the table for me to take a seat.

"I have skills," he says with a grin before turning his attention back to the stove. "Are you feeling better this morning, *lyubimaya*?"

Sweetheart. Little one. Wife. I wonder why he barely ever calls me by my name now like he did when we were only friends, but not enough to risk displeasing him by asking. Ultimately, even though they are all his ways of claiming me, they are also terms of endearment, and I know he means all of them in a good way.

It's not anyone's fault my feelings don't equal his, nor that he's aware of this, and we're now in a marriage where we must get along. If I can't love him, I can, at least, give him the things he desires and requires from me if only to keep things in a proper place between us. "Yes, I am. Thank you, husband."

"Glad to hear it." Separating the food on two plates, he walks toward the table and sets one down in front of me, and taking a seat across from me. "I hope that isn't too much for you. On my own, I would eat all this myself."

Picking up my fork, I shake my head and press down on the center of my egg to make the yolk run. "It looks delicious. Even the most single man must be able to feed himself, husband."

Both of us eat our food while it's hot in relative silence, and once I've pushed my plate away after finishing, I stare out the window and wait for him. And for instructions, because I'm sure he has things he wants to do and will make me do with him.

"Look at me, *lyubimaya*." He swallows hard when my gaze reaches his as he puts down his fork, the gentleness more in tune with my friend rather than my husband, as well as…remorse? "Last night showed me I've been too hard on you. For many years, we have been friends and there's no reason for me to treat you as I have since our engagement. I enjoy many things I have ached to show you and want for you to take pleasure in as well. That doesn't include making you sick over it or making you fear me."

"I know, husband."

His apology is surprising, but I do know he's

honest at this moment because of the sadness etched on his face. Maksim isn't a bad man for his desires any more than O was; the difference is, there hadn't been a past between or a friendship with O. There had only been a lust that had begun the moment our eyes met in that restaurant.

But I have to forget O and find joy with Maksim, my husband. He may have pushed too hard, but if O — the man who took me against my will and kept me locked in a room — were doing these things with me, would I be this upset and resentful? Something tells me no, I wouldn't be fighting against it hard, or maybe even at all; the rejection I felt at being made to leave proves the latter likely.

I liked what he did to me, and that means I have been unfair, making it my turn to feel ashamed at my own resentment-filled behavior. "I don't fear you, Maksim. And I think our busy wedding day plus the food on the plane and being tired...it wasn't good."

His eyes flash when I say his name, but he doesn't rebuke me, only frowns more. "Don't treat my poor behavior as nothing. However, we're married now and both of us must put our best into it. I promise you I'll do better in many things from now on, but you need to do the same, especially if we are to have a family one day."

"I agree, but..." Lifting one hand to my neck, I rub the choker as my eyes fill with tears, especially at the hoop now hanging in the pendant's place. "I don't like wearing this."

Standing up, he holds out a hand and draws me to my feet when I place mine in his, and kisses my lips softly. "My job as your husband is to take care of you, love you and any children we have, and protect you. Not only is this choker meant to declare you as mine, but the intricate design is also to fool people into thinking it nothing more than expensive jewelry, and hides the fact you can be tracked with it. It is necessary."

"Protect me from what? And why would you need me to wear something that will track—"

His eyes are intense when he covers my mouth with the palm of his hand. "Do you trust me? Do you believe me a man of honor?"

My answer is muffled underneath his hand, but still honest. "Yes."

"I can't tell you anything except there are many in this world who aren't trustworthy; men who think nothing of hurting women to get what they want. Your father does business with many of them, and upon our return, I will be involved in this more, as the man who will take over for your father. Because of it, I will not take any chances when it comes to the woman I love."

I want to argue, to ask why he and my father work with these men if they are so dangerous, and why I'm the one who must be punished for their choices. Instead, I let the emotions tumbling around inside me show on my face even as I nod, and he strokes my lips with his thumb before smiling softly.

"However, while we are here, I will remove it at night when we're inside for the evening, as long as you don't complain or cry in the mornings about having to wear it again. Only here," he says sternly at my bright and happy smile. "It goes back on before we head home, *lyubimaya*, and I will hear no more of it. Understand?"

May not be what I want, but a compromise is better than his unyielding demands. "Yes."

"Yes what, *zhena*?"

His question is as playful as the look in his eyes, and because he isn't expecting it, I whirl in his arms before taking off at an equally playful jog through the suite.

When he traps me in a corner of the bedroom, dominant Maksim takes me over his knee to spank me for not addressing him properly, but it's the sweet friendly version of him that bares every inch of me and makes kind, unhurried love to me for the first time.

6

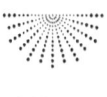

OWEN

"THIS IS FOOLISH." Isaac doesn't mince words, glaring at me from where he sits behind his desk. "You know you are risking your life by returning to Russia for this woman, correct?"

"Yes."

"You ignore my warning the first time about watching your back and now you want to go back there again after Dorokhov warned you to stay away? Do you have a death wish?"

"No." I can say more but no need. He's speaking more than enough for both of us and I have a headache from a late night of trying to iron out the details of a good plan — that would be the one he's currently deriding.

"I disagree. There is no way you will be able to get near her. I would bet my own life everyone has been warned to keep an eye out for you."

Simone, eyes wide during this whole

conversation as she sits in the other chair next to me, nods her head as I glance at her. "I'll say the same thing."

"What is your suggestion then, hm?" My question is directed at Isaac as I stand up and walk to look out the window. "I returned four weeks ago. They will return any day from wherever the hell they went, if they haven't already, and I've got all the information I need to know about Aristov's life and financials."

I understand their worries, but it isn't as if there are many options available here. Sure, it'll be risky to show up at her door when he's not home. However, I don't plan on being stupid and walking right up to the front door without making sure she'll be the one answering it.

"From where I am sitting, you have two options. You can forget about her and save yourself as well as her the potential grief your interference may cost."

Not even bothering to look at him, I lift my left hand and give him the middle finger, feeling a slight satisfaction when Simone laughs softly.

Isaac isn't amused, of course, but goes on to say, "The other is to send someone else there in your place. Someone inconspicuous, who can spend some time there and find a way into her life to gain her trust, and find out whether she wants to leave or not."

"And who the hell do we know and trust who'll do that? A person who knows Russian and can spend weeks or even months there, unrecognized?" He meets my question with silence. "Exactly why I'm—"

"I'll do it."

Both Isaac and I turn to look at Simone, my face filled with curiosity as to why she would offer, while his face screams 'I don't fucking think so' loud and clear as he remarks, "Absolutely not."

"But—"

"Fuck no, *min elskede*. It is dangerous and I will not put you in harm's way for him." He stabs a finger in my direction even though his gaze doesn't leave her face. "Why would you offer anyway? You don't speak Russian."

"I don't. But contrary to what you two think, that makes me the perfect candidate." When he opens his mouth to object, she holds up a finger to let her finish and smiles. "I can take a course over there to learn Russian and making friends with her may be more likely with someone closer in age."

"She's got a point."

If Isaac were the type of man to strangle someone to death, his irate expression tells me my name would be near the top of his shit list. "I am not sending my wife to Russia on her own, for you to interfere in the life of a woman who may not even want to leave, let alone be with you."

Standing up, she walks over to stand in front of him behind the desk, and when she crouches down, I avert my gaze back out the window while continuing to listen to their conversation. "Let's go as a family. We've all got passports and you've promised me we would take a trip but there was the pregnancy and then the wedding. Think of it as our belated honeymoon."

Fuck, she's laying it on thick, but if she were asking me…yeah, I would give in to her too. Something about those big beautiful eyes of hers…she's not mine, but I would still do anything for her if she asked me too. How the hell he resists her sometimes is beyond my understanding.

"You would rather go to Russia for a honeymoon than say, Bermuda? Punta Cana? Cancun?"

The destination isn't the problem; her wanting to help me is. He only tolerates me for her and just as I'm about to say it doesn't matter because I'm fucking going to help Ramona myself, my phone rings, and Joy's name flashes on the screen.

Isaac and Simone's voices lower as I answer the call with a smile. "Joy."

"Owen." She sounds tired and worn out, and I wonder if she's been having trouble sleeping again. "You're going to be so pissed."

"Oh? Why?"

"Your visa to go back to Russia was denied. Says you're banned from entering for five years."

I don't even ask why. I know why, and who, and can also appreciate the humor in being banned from my own home country even though I'm exactly as pissed as she said I would be. "Son of a...that fucker."

"I know. But how? I mean, he has that much power?"

"He's an arms dealer, Joy. He supplies the weapons — and fuck knows what else — and bribes his way through everything. Everybody has their price and even the government will do what you want if there's something big enough in it for them."

"You can't get over there now. What are you going to do?"

Looking over to find Isaac and Simone staring at me with an interest in my conversation, the suggestion I give is one they'll all object to, and it's pure manipulation because my options are really limited now without breaking the law. "They banned Owen Chandler. So, I guess I will obtain a third identity for myself and hope I don't get fucking busted."

"Owen—"

Isaac's sudden smile as Simone's whispers in his ear intrigues me, cutting off Joy because while she means well, I'm not up for listening to a lecture when we both know I won't change my mind. "Joy, I'll be home in a bit. Go get some rest, you sound exhausted."

"Okay." She sighs, resigned to the inevitable choice I'll make. "See you then."

Hanging up, I slip the phone into my pocket along with my hands and turn to face them. "Are you amused by my dilemma or something else?"

"I will not tolerate you being arrested for possessing false documents. And not because I care what happens to you, but because the last thing I want is Simone sobbing over another man as he languishes in a foreign prison."

"Your concern is touching, as usual."

Simone laughs. "Stop it, you two. Owen, from everything you said, this woman might not be in danger, but it doesn't mean she's in that marriage of her own free will. And we all care about free will here, even Isaac. Her father is afraid of you getting near his daughter to the point you've been banned to prevent you from coming back for her. That alone makes it imperative someone makes sure Ramona is given the opportunity to leave if she wants it."

"Thank you." My gratitude is directed at Isaac even though she's saying the words because without him none of this would happen at all. "I am more than willing to go great lengths for her, but it won't do either of us any good if I'm locked up or killed in the process."

Isaac takes Simone's hand in his and rises from his chair with a derisive snort, his disagreement with that statement clear although he doesn't say it. "I shall get everything in order for Simone's schooling as a front and then apply for our visas. I imagine it will take four to six weeks to set things in motion and our exact arrival will depend on the course schedule."

"Fuck. I know these things take time, but four to six weeks minimum?"

"A plan such as this with the intention of ingratiating ourselves into the lives of this woman must be well thought out. We know Aristov followed her here even though he knew they were going to marry, might be aware something went on between the two of you, and undoubtedly keeps her protected at all times from the business aspect alone." When I curse and turn toward the window, he continues, albeit in a kinder tone. "You must trust this is the best course of action. Even having her watched until we arrive is impossible since we have no idea who we can rely on."

Basically, sit tight for now. Then, let them go to Russia to take care of this because my hands are legally tied, and means I'll spend the next few months wondering if she's all right or not.

"You're not going to punch me if it's a waste of time, are you?" I don't want to imagine that as the outcome, but being blind to reality isn't smart.

"No," Simone says softly. "We get a trip and a new experience as a family, among other things. I trust your instincts; they haven't steered me wrong yet."

"Yes, well, let's hope it remains that way."

"It will."

Nodding, I turn to the door. "Thank you again. I'll see myself out." And think about all the ways I can torture Dorokhov if I ever get my hands on him.

"I will be in touch," Isaac informs me, but I don't look back thanks to the sound of Simone's muted squeak of surprise. "Shut the door behind you."

Grateful as I am for their assistance, their undisguised happiness doesn't annoy me for once. Instead, the sharp prick of jealousy in my chest or wanting what they have makes me curse as I head outside.

The drive home is long. When I finally head to my room after a drink, I find Joy curled up in my bed sound asleep, and pass out minutes after joining her.

"Owen?"

Why is she talking? I put a gag in her mouth just so she couldn't talk and distract me, but when I look at her it's gone and she's jabbing me in the stomach with something.

"Owen, let me up or I'm going to piss all over your bed, and that's neither your kink or mine."

Watersports? I had no idea Ramona knew what those were, but she's right, not my thing.

My eyes fly open at the sharp sting of a slap in my face, and Joy's angry gaze stares at me from where I've climbed on top of her as I dreamt.

"Fuck." Rolling off her, the harsh morning light assaults my eyes, and I cover them with my arm while the bed dips as she gets up. "Sorry."

"No worries," she mumbles. "Be right back."

The door to the bathroom attached to my room — the one Ramona showered in — opens and shuts, and just as dozing off again seems like a good possibility, I hear Joy…crying?

Stilling, I listen to make sure that's what the sound is before sitting up, stretching while rising to my feet. Walking over, the crying gets more distinct, and nothing makes me love technology more than not having to beg her to open the door. Placing my hand on the pad, the door slides open and reveals Joy sitting on the floor with her head buried in her hands.

"Go away," she wails, but her protest is weak and unconvincing.

Without saying a word, I crouch down and gather her in my arms, carrying her back to bed and placing her in the center of it before grabbing a tissue. She takes it, turns to face away from me, and blows her nose before whispering, "I wanted to cry in private."

"Then you shouldn't have done it in my bathroom."

She laughs weakly, clearly against her will, and turns back to where I stand next to the bed, her face filled with misery even as her cheeks flush. "I...well, you turned over and started touching me. I didn't realize you were asleep until you said her name...and I shouldn't have slapped you for it."

"It worked, didn't it?"

"Yeah, but...you've never...we've never." Her face burns brighter as she takes a deep breath and lets it out slowly, but speaks before I can put her any further embarrassment. "I...I should've known you weren't aware from that fact alone."

I try not to smile and fail. "So are you upset because I tried to fuck you in my sleep, Joy, or because it wasn't you my brain thought I was about to fuck?"

The level of red: flaming. Tells me everything I need to know as she rolls away and off the bed, stalking over to the tiny wastebasket to throw the tissue away before whirling to glare at me. "Both. And I shouldn't be. God, I've known you since you were sixteen. Playing and doing a scene are different than...than..."

"Fucking me." I fill in the blanks for her, and perhaps I shouldn't be enjoying this, but I'm a man. Joy wants to fuck me; she thinks meeting me when I was a minor is a deterrent eighteen years later? "We're adults, Joy. You feel shame where there shouldn't be any. Neither me nor my cock is withering at the idea of fucking you."

"Oh my god!"

She'll be forty this year and still blushes like a schoolgirl. Excellent.

Grinning unrepentantly, I point at her shorts and tank, locking my eyes with hers. "Take off your clothes and kneel."

Balling her fists at her side, she shakes her head, but I give her a minute to process this sudden change of direction just as I had in the car after my return.

"Did you come up with a different solution last night? Or are you going anyway?" The way she fights her desire is impressive, lifting her chin while defiance shines from her eyes and in her stance, all while she changes topics to gain distance from the unwanted feelings. "If you are then—"

"We'll discuss that later. You need to do as you were told, Joy. Now."

Her removal of her tank and shorts takes longer than it should, but by the time I'm standing in front of her, she's on her knees in the position she knows well. But it isn't good for what I want to do, so grabbing her hair and twisting it around my hand, I tug it tight so she knows not to look up at me.

"Up a little, spread your legs, and touch yourself for me like you do when you're all alone."

Even as she obeys, the trail of her hand down her stomach is slow, and the shakiness in her voice gives away how nervous she is. "Owen—"

A sharp, quick tug is all it takes to cut her off while her hands slip between her thighs, her eyes squeezed shut. "That's 'sir' to you, but you won't need it because I don't want you to speak. Just feel."

Watching her hand slide back and forth between her legs, it's tempting to say nothing else and see how frustrated she becomes, but she wanted this so I'll give it to her.

"Fuck yourself, Joy. One finger, and then two. Good girl." She moans, lifting up and down a little as she rides her own hand, all her inhibitions sliding away with each second that passes. "You wish you were fucking my cock instead of those inadequate fingers of yours, don't you?"

"Mmm."

Shoving my shorts down with my free hand, I step out of them before fisting my dick and putting it near her lips, murmuring, "Open your eyes, Joy."

Lips parting as she catches sight of my cock, she licks them and bucks against her hand with a soft moan.

"Come for me. Get yourself off for me like a good girl and I'll let you suck me off as a reward. Use another finger if you need to."

Her eyes gleam with the promise an instant

before she slams them shut again, her whole body shaking as she comes hard, and her cry of pleasure is cut off when I push my dick past her lips, rewarding her with more than promised.

After, as we lie in bed with her curled up against me while our bodies cool, her words are soft and sad when she says, "I didn't say anything because I didn't want things to change between us."

"And they haven't. It's just sex. Isn't that what you told me yourself?"

"Yes, but I wasn't referring to me and you, since I didn't expect this to happen."

She slides off me as I turn to my side, studying her with interest because I don't like the guilt I hear in her words. "Then what are you talking about?"

"We work together. No woman you're with seriously is going to be okay with the fact we work together and now we can't even deny that we slept together at some point."

"I see." Leaning in, I gently kiss her on the mouth and say firmly, "Even though I understand why you feel this way about it, we are both single. We haven't done anything that is the business of anyone except us, including future partners."

She blinks as if surprised I would put my mouth on hers, hand coming up to touch her lips as she attempts to protest. "But—"

"No." When I do it again to stop her from

talking about it, she whimpers and leans into the kiss, deciding on what we do next with her simple action. "No more talking."

There are no further protests from her after that, and I'm glad to have something to do besides dread the yawning months ahead of me.

7

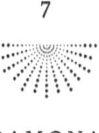

RAMONA

MAKSIM KEPT his promise for the rest of our honeymoon. Outside the bedroom, he acted more like the kind and caring typical gentleman that men are in Russia, making sure all my needs and many of my wants were taken care of. This way benefited his dominance in the bedroom, my submission was less forced and as a result, the sex became more enjoyable for both of us.

Now, after being home for only a day, I actually miss being alone with him, doing nothing besides spending time together exploring and getting comfortable with each other in a daily way.

A month of spending every moment with him means being home by myself feels strange. He woke up early, got ready for the day as I made him breakfast, and left me with a kiss after saying he was going to work. My job and entire future from now on? Housewife and mother, as I've always expected it to become one day.

Last night, we walked into a freshly dusted home, a kitchen stocked with food, and a pile of accumulated mail on the table — courtesy of Maksim's mother. This morning, Maksim opened the mail before work, handing me cards connected to his bank and credit accounts for my personal use, and told me not only to go visit my mother but to take her shopping with me as well.

I don't need anything; I have more than enough clothing and personal items, all delivered and put away while we were gone. But it's better to go spend even a little money as not doing so will offend him since he's providing for me.

When my mother opens the door, she lets me inside and shuts it before turning to me, pulling me into her tight embrace. But if I thought she wouldn't notice, wouldn't comment, it's only because I've been in denial and hoped to stay that way for awhile.

The tears in her eyes as she pulls back say otherwise, her voice quavering as she murmurs, "I am going to be a *babushka*."

"I need to take a test." My own eyes water, but out of distress instead of happiness like her. "I'm not sure…"

More like I want to pretend I'm not.

"I am, but of course, we must find out." She pats my hand, drawing me into the living room toward the couch, making sure I'm sitting before grabbing her purse. "You stay here and I will be right back."

She starts to walk away, stopping when I ask, "How did you know, Mama?"

"You are my daughter. I know you well." Her gaze drops down my body to my chest with a laugh. "Your body is already changing. Rest. I won't be gone long."

Lying down as she leaves, I wonder when she will realize my body shouldn't be changing this early.

Only a month married to Maksim, we had sex for the first time only six weeks ago, and I haven't had my period since before my arrival in America.

Even if everything that went on delayed ovulation until Maksim and I began having sex, I would be what? Maybe five weeks? I know all about sex and babies and the timeline for changes in a woman's body during pregnancy doesn't add up for that.

That's why I've been in denial because a little over eight weeks ago I had sex with Owen and I don't remember him using a condom as he did the first time at my place. The timing there is more likely.

Oh god, what the hell am I going to do if this baby isn't Maksim's? He's my husband, this is our life together now, but I won't lie to him. And he may not be hurt or care; it's not as if we were together.

A ton of other questions run through my mind, including ones about how to tell Owen, all of which are shoved to the side as she comes through the front door with a huge grin on her face. Taking the test out of the bag, she hands it to me and shoos me out of the room.

Five minutes later, I show her the positive test and say, "Let me talk to Maksim and tell him first. Before you share, please?"

Smiling she takes my hands in hers and nods. "Naturally. Maksim will be excited, just as he said on your wedding day. And I saw your surprise earlier but don't worry darling. My body changed early as well and chances are you are like me. Nothing to get upset or fret over."

"Really?"

She squeezes my hands in reassurance, her eyes brimming with joy. "Yes. Eat right and take care of yourself. Like right now. You look fatigued, probably from all that travel. Go get some rest and ring me later after you tell him. And congratulations dear."

Thinking about what she said while driving home, a part of me is torn between hoping my mothers comments about the changes are genetic while another wants the baby to be Owen's no matter the consequences.

Preoccupied, my key is turned in the lock and about to open the door when I see a dark-tinted SUV park down the street, similar or perhaps exactly like the one I'm pretty sure drove behind me the whole way here.

Maksim's warning ringing in my ears, I hurry inside and slam the door shut behind me. My entire body shakes uncontrollably as I stumble toward the bathroom, my stomach rolling, in the same way it has every morning for weeks now, and makes me glad today's the last day I'll have to deal with it alone.

When Maksim arrives home, I am sitting on the couch watching TV. He grins at me, studying from where he stands in the doorway with his arms crossed and leaning against the frame.

The happiness and affection on his face are too much for me, especially with what I have to tell him, and I burst into tears while spitting out the words. "Maksim…I'm pregnant."

"I know, *lyubimaya*. How are you feeling?"

"What do you mean you know? Did my mother tell you after she said she wouldn't?"

He laughs and walks closer. "No. I figured it out many weeks ago. You really believe you were quiet when getting sick every morning? You have many talents, *moya prekrasnaya zhena*, but vomiting discreetly isn't one a person usually possesses."

"Why didn't you say something?"

"I didn't wish to upset you." He sits down and

cuddles me in his arms, stroking my back before kissing the top of my head, and sighs. "I knew you might not deal with it well and waited until you were ready on your own."

Taking a deep breath, my words are unsteady even as his soothing caresses are working to help me calm me down. "Maksim...I need to tell you something. I...it might hurt you and—"

"Shh. Relax, *malyshka*. Getting upset isn't good for you or the baby."

God, the way he cares makes my heart hurt. "It's important—"

"No." Moving his hand to grasp my chin, he makes me look him in the eyes while keeping my body held tight against his. "Listen to me. We are having a baby, Ramona. This baby is mine and yours, and you will say it is so. Are we clear?"

The fierceness of his gaze, the way he's phrased the words, and the deliberate use of my name click with his statement about dealing well with the pregnancy, and then I'm crying because he knows. Has known for a while, perhaps even as far back as the trip, and has been preparing me for this moment with his warnings.

Shoving the words past my sobs, I croak out, "How?"

"You think your father would let you travel to America without someone keeping an eye on you? I wanted to stop you because I knew nothing good would come of your involvement with Chandler, and I thought you safe to leave alone that night. I never took him for a man who would do as he did."

I should've known and perhaps, deep down, I did know. My sobs subside while the tears keep flowing down my cheeks. "He didn't hurt me, Maksim. I was a willing participant. He let me decide both times."

He clenches his jaw and glances away, the muscles there ticking twice before he looks at me again. "Good. I will punch him one less time than planned if I ever see him again."

I bet he would and if I weren't so upset, I would laugh a little at what he said. "Maksim, does Papa...know?"

Grimacing, he moves his hand from my chin to cup my cheek and speaks against my lips after a soft kiss. "Yes, *malyshka*, he knows about your time there and what happened. This is why you will lie through your teeth when he questions the pregnancy. Your privacy means nothing to your papa and neither does mine."

Whispering, I don't keep the newly spiraling fear from my voice. "Do I want to know what happens if I tell the truth?"

He shakes his head with no hesitation, his gaze haunted and regretful as he draws away a little. "No."

My heart aches as if I've been stabbed in it and, terrified for all the possible horror his one word invokes, I nod and ask, "What will I tell him?"

"You will be frank and tell him protection was used; you are positive the baby is mine. That we slept together the night after your return, once you agreed to the engagement and we went out to dinner."

Close enough to the eight weeks estimate and lends credit to the lie. He's thought this through, something I am glad for because I truly had no idea what I was going to tell my papa when he found out.

And because I'm finally getting more of the big picture here — even if I don't know details — I sigh and place my hand over the one he has on my cheek. "That SUV is going to follow me everywhere, isn't it."

"Yes, *lyubimaya*, we're never alone, and you never were before. You just never had a reason to notice."

"I see."

The idea of lying makes me want to cry and throw up even more. I want to talk to Owen, to tell him he's going to have a child with me. Maybe he won't care; maybe he'll dismiss me and tell me it's my problem to deal with. I don't know. I barely knew the man and now we're going to be tied together forever even if he doesn't know it.

Maksim pulls me away from my thoughts with a rough capture of my lips, kissing me as if he wants to drown in me, get lost in me. But there's a tinge of desperation to it as if he's trying to convince me of something, and when he pulls my back, the anguish in my heart grows tenfold at his unmistakable despair.

"Your father has plans, and nothing, no-one, will get in the way of what he wants. I know what you're thinking and I promise you, it will not turn out well if you attempt to contact him. Be glad your father wanted us to marry, for he could've chosen someone else among his connections, and you wouldn't have wanted that."

The truth, the one he's been telling me for weeks, tumbles out between us. "My father isn't a good man, is he?"

Swallowing hard, he gazes down at me with pain in his eyes and says, "He is good to those who do as they're told."

"And you?"

"I am a good man who would rather take over for your father than let the business fall into anyone else's hands."

"Why? If you could walk away, why didn't you?"

"For you. To protect you because your father will never let you go willingly."

The fact he is as trapped as me makes me sad. "He was never going to let me marry Odin, was he?"

"No, *lyubimaya*. Never."

Which means my father lied about lying to me.

If any tears were left in me, I would cry; for me, for Maksim, and for the innocent life inside me. And for Owen, because my lie will protect him and save his life while keeping his own flesh and blood from him.

Nodding at Maksim, I wrap my arms around his neck and whisper into his ear when he tightens his embrace. "Okay. I'll do what needs to be done."

His relief is palpable but there isn't any relief for me. Just heartache and shame at what my life has become, and sensing it will only get worse from here.

In the end, I close my eyes and ask for the one thing I may never deserve from Owen if he finds out.

Forgive me.

8

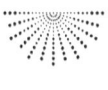

OWEN

It's the first week of June, and three months have passed since Isaac and Simone agreed to go to Russia. They, along with their two sons, as well as Helen and Jim, left a week ago on one flight, while the security detail Isaac hired took a trip the few days before that to set up for their arrival.

Simone agreed to let me know when she actually comes in contact with Ramona, and so far, she's only sent me emails detailing the beginning of her Russian language courses, and how much they are all enjoying themselves.

I'm happy everything's going smoothly; not so thrilled with how long this whole situation is taking. I am quickly running out of patience and can't do a damn thing about it.

"Owen." Joy's voice rings out from where she stands in the doorway leading into the office at the restaurant, pointing at her wrist when I lift my head from where I'm staring at my computer screen. "Nearly two in the morning. We should head home."

"All right. Just give me another minute or two."

"Sure. I'll wait for you in the car."

She leaves, closing the door behind her, and as I press the button on the monitor to turn it off after shutting down the computer, my phone rings in my pocket.

Thinking an impatient Joy is calling to get my attention, I answer the phone without looking at the screen and put it up to my ear. "I'm on my way."

"To Russia? You're banned, remember?"

Simone's laugh is perfect and couldn't have come at a more perfect time. I respond with a chuckle of my own and slip into my suit jacket. "I answered without looking at my caller ID."

"That's all right. I know it's late, but you told me to call you immediately and—"

That stops me in my tracks, the door leading out of the office halfway open. "You saw her?"

"Yes, in the supermarket on the way to class, but that's it."

"And?"

Her pause is long, to the point I'm about to see if we lost connection when she clears her throat and finally speaks again. "She's fine, Owen. Looked perfectly healthy and...and happy. I was briefly in the same aisle as they were, tried to look as if I was engrossed in looking for what I wanted while sneaking glances, but the second time I caught her husband staring at me."

"Did this occur this morning?"

"Yes. About thirty minutes ago."

"Are you sure it was Aristov? In a store at ten a.m. instead of work on a weekday?"

"Positive. We have pictures, remember? They were standing quite close and when she looked up at him while he stared at me, she didn't even try to see what he was focused on. Just lifted her hand to his face to get his attention, and kissed him when he shifted his eyes back to her. Then, he leaned in, whispered in her ear, and they walked off with their groceries, laughing."

Of course. Why would I expect to hear anything except how normal her life is? Anything less won't fly in public; the only way Simone's going to know anything more than superficial is by befriending her.

"He's a Russian man. Many are shameless flirts." Scoffing with disgust, I exit the office and lock the door, heading to the main door as she laughs on the other end. "I'm serious, Simone. He probably would've hit on you if she hadn't been there."

"Oh, I've already been hit on by quite a few men since arriving here, just while walking and even with the kids! Brazen behavior, but honestly, it's kinda flattering too."

"Careful. You don't want Isaac to lock you up in his beautiful Russian dungeon, do you?"

"Shut up."

I love the smile in her voice. "Thanks for calling. We know she's alive and well, at least, which is more than we knew before."

"Yep. And hey, I think you should know…"

The phone suddenly crackles, whatever Simone is saying becoming unintelligible, and after a few seconds, the connection dies.

Growling with frustration, I try to call her back. When that effort is met with dead air, I shove the phone back in my pocket, lock up the restaurant, and return to waiting for her to call me.

Joy slides into my lap the moment the car starts moving and makes it easy to forget everything except the feel of her soft body wrapped in my arms.

"STARING AT YOUR PHONE WON'T MAKE IT RING."

"I know." Reaching over to place it on the nightstand, my phone clatters against the surface as I make a silent vow not to look at it again before morning. "Surprised she hasn't called back after we were cut off last night."

"Mmhm. She's probably busy." Joy sits up and straddles my lap, placing her hands flat on my chest as she grinds her lower body against mine. "Let me take your mind off it for a little while, hon."

"Fuck, I never would've taken you for a nympho."

Taking my cock in her hand, she lifts her body and poises the tip at the entrance to her pussy, letting go to slide down on me with a moan. "I'm just getting it while you're giving it to me, sir. I also have years of a dry spell to make up for."

My fingers dig into her hips as she rides my dick at a pace meant to drive both of us to the point of madness and enjoying every minute of it. When her pussy clenches around me, her surprised gasp of pleasure and fingers dig into my chest as she comes, and I roll her onto her back.

She clings to me as I fuck her with the hard, fast thrusts we both prefer, and with a final plunge to bury myself deep inside her enough to get lost, she screams and arches her back, her nails digging into my shoulders as we both orgasm with a near savage intensity.

Rolling off her, we lay side by side breathing hard like we just ran a marathon, and she cuddles up against me once we've cooled down. Resting a hand on her back, I start to caress up and down her spine with the tips of my fingers, and release a chuckle when she shivers.

"Owen?"

"Hm?"

"I need to find a man."

Gathering what she means, I tease her anyway because it's the perfect opening. "Ouch. Not the right thing to say to a man after he makes you scream like that."

"Comical as always. You know that's not what I meant."

Some of my amusement dissipates at hearing the sadness in her voice even though she doesn't pull away. "I'm sorry, I know you're serious. Why do you need to find a man, Joy?"

"I want a husband and children. I'll be forty soon. It may be too late for children of my own by the time I find a man I want them with, but—"

"That's bullshit. Science is amazing Joy, and if you wish to be a mother, then you should be. And you don't need a man for that other than the obvious."

"Yes, I know. That's an option, sure, but I suppose part of me always wanted the traditional family ideal, and my children to have two parents who love them and work together."

Pressing a kiss to the top of her head, the sound of her sigh makes me smile, and clasp her as close as I can to convey my sincerity. "You would be a terrific mother, Joy, so if that's what you want, go for it with a man or no man. Two parents is excellent, but so is one. One or two beats out zero any day."

"I'll keep that in mind. Thanks." With a yawn,

she rests her hand on the center of my chest and relaxes against me. "Night, Owen. Try to get some sleep. You aren't useful to anyone if you're falling over from lack of rest."

"Hush, unless you want me to roll you over right now and see how much cock your ass can take."

"Ugh. Goodnight for sure."

Anal is a hard limit for Joy, who seems to enjoy nearly everything I throw her way, and my inability to sleep has me pondering ways I can persuade her to give it a try.

And although I eventually fall asleep, it's the sleep of a man who is waiting for a phone call he doesn't want to miss, and once again, I get a poor night's rest because of it.

I RARELY FEEL SOMETHING BAD IS OR WILL BE happening, and had always scoffed when someone said they 'just knew' or 'had an inkling something was off.' But after waking up around noon three days later, I eat breakfast and hop in the shower, only managing to wash my hair before getting the sudden inexplicable urge to talk to Joy.

Shutting off the water, I step out and don't even bother drying off before exiting the bathroom. My phone rings at the same time Joy bursts through the door with tears streaming down her cheeks, pointing at my phone as she grabs my laptop off the nearby table. "Answer it!"

My phone is on the nightstand, and seeing Joy's tears along with Simone's name flashing on the screen, grabbing and answering my phone and putting it up to my ears feel like it takes forever.

"Owen." Simone sobs over the crackling line. "I'm so sorry. I…I've been trying to call you for two days—"

"I can barely understand you, Simone. What the hell's wrong and why are you sorry? The connection sucks."

"She's…she's dead," she wails, my heart thumping hard in response, denial rearing its head because she can't be talking about the woman she was sent there to save if necessary. "The day I called you? That night, there was a shooting and a fire…and—"

The line cuts out, and I drop the phone as Joy sets the laptop on the bed and turns it to face me. She's pulled up the local news channel for Saint Petersburg, ugly pictures flashing at me on the screen while she turns the sound up, and the sudden roaring grows louder in my ears as the reporters words assault every fucking bit of me.

"The deadly shooting happened at a downtown warehouse in what appears as retaliation for a business deal turned ugly and set aflame by the

time emergency services arrived following reports
of shots fired.

The owner of the warehouse, Ivan Dorokhov, as
well as his daughter, Ramona — who was
approximately 22 weeks pregnant according to her
mother — and her husband, Maksim Aristov, are
among those confirmed dead. Attempts are being
made to identify the other ten victims.

There are no suspects at this time and police
encourage…"

Murdered.

Twenty-two weeks. Five and a half months
along. I run the time through my head and that
means January.

Mid-January, when I had her locked up in that
fucking room before sending her away without
saying goodbye.

The child had been *mine* and now they are
both dead.

Slamming my eyes shut, the roaring in my ears
becomes unbearable, and the last thing I
remember is Joy yelling my name as the thought
of someone murdering Ramona and my child
brings me to my knees.

PART II
WHAT DOESN'T KILL YOU

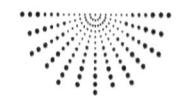

9

RAMONA

Tomorrow will be two years in hiding.

Maksim told me running had become the only option and sent me packing with a new identity — Veronika Barinova, precisely — and enough money in a foreign bank account with the same name to keep me worry free. So scared I would be caught unlike the first time I traveled under a fake name; perhaps innocent had been bliss then. This time I was glad my pregnancy gave me the excuse needed for my nerves the whole trip.

The immigration officers never blinked, though. And upon landing, the last one went through my papers, smiled, and welcomed me to my new home in the USA.

I still don't know how Maksim managed it all, but if there's one thing I learned while married to him, it was to not ask questions unless the answer was something I genuinely wished to hear. And at the time, I wouldn't have truly listened anyway; I know that now, at least.

The beautiful house I bought after arriving with the money Maksim gave me is private — my closest neighbor is a little less than a mile away — while still being close enough to a city to shop and everything else. I've been waiting for Maksim to come as he promised he would, and my hope he hadn't truly died in that fire lessens with each day that passes. He told me not to believe everything I heard and read, to focus on building a new life for the baby and me, but it's hard after this long not to wonder more and more.

My home, my family, and him — that's what I miss the most. Unsure if my father is truly dead or not, even though the fire actually occurred, that is one truth I wish to know.

And my poor Mama, who believes me dead and will never know otherwise. No coming back from that which means even if my family is alive, going to Russia to see them probably won't ever be an option I have.

My life isn't bad, but it still traps me because I'm not free, and something tells me I won't ever be truly free again.

"Katya!" I walk toward my daughter, reaching her just as she's about to shove a rock from the gravel driveway in her mouth, and sweep her up into my arms with a laugh. "You can't eat rocks, sweetie."

She whines as I take the rock from her hand and toss it on the ground, then giggles when I distract her by twirling around in a circle with a soft, "Whee!"

When we stop, she looks up at me with a happy grin, and all I see in the chubby-cheeked face of my little girl with her golden blonde curls and bright green eyes is her father. A double dose of pain in those moments at night when she's sound asleep in her bed and I'm all alone in mine.

At nineteen months, she's my greatest joy, and the reason I've stayed hidden even as the choking fear that we'll be isolated from the world forever creeps in. We've been safe here and after everything that's gone on, safety in what I have here is my security blanket.

Katya snuggles against me, sticking her thumb in her mouth and closing her eyes, a clear indication the time has come for her mid-day nap. Carrying her inside, I engage the slide lock on the door — something I always did when we first moved here and has become habit — and head to her bedroom to lay her down.

But as I bend over and start to place her on it, she tugs her thumb out of her mouth and throws her arms around my neck. "No! Mama bed!"

"You know the rules. You sleep in your bed, sweetie. Big girls sleep in their own bed." Hers is a convertible crib that turned into a toddler bed, a changeover I made after she kept managing to almost climb out of it, and has a safety railing in front. "Mama's jealous of your bed. It's very comfy."

She lets me put her down as I say that, and sits staring up at me for a moment. Then, her little grin again, patting the bed next to her as she reaches over to grab her stuffed bunny. "You sweep."

"Aw, baby, mama's too big for your bed." Leaning over, I kiss her on the cheek as she lays down and cuddles her bunny with a pout. "Make bunny sleep, he's tired!"

My big, exaggerated yawn while straightening up again makes her giggling, but then her eyes begin to drift shut as she sucks on her thumb again. Bad habit from what I've read, but she's already doing it less than a few months ago so I've just let it go because she'll grow out of it.

Shutting her door until it's only open a crack, I head into the living room to use my quiet time wisely — reading and eating food that isn't cut up into tiny pieces in case Katya wants me to share.

THE SOUND OF A CAR DOOR SHUTTING STARTLES me out my impromptu nap. Sitting up and rubbing my eyes, I glance at the clock my phone and gasp, shocked that I've been sleeping for nearly an hour.

Katya's soft and even breathing through the monitor is a relief and a surprise as well — she usually doesn't nap this long — but I will enjoy the extra time for myself after determining who's outside.

Frowning, I turn to the window and carefully peek through the blinds, my mouth drying at the sight of a gleaming black car parked in my driveway right behind mine. My urge to hide and not answer the door disappears the moment the car door opens and someone I know better than anyone else in the world steps out.

Backing away, I slip into my sandals and smooth my hand down my blouse as if it will matter, and then unlock the door. Opening it and stepping into the opening, I let out a joyous cry and take off at a run, jumping into Maksim's arms the moment he opens them.

He wraps them around me tightly, hugging me like only a Russian man with an abundance of passion can, but I don't care that he's crushing me — as long as he doesn't let me go. Burying my face in the crook of his neck, he strokes the back of my head as I cling to him, incoherent and sobbing with relief.

"Shh, *lyubimaya*," he murmurs softly in his strongly accented English, keeping a hold of me around the waist as he begins walking toward the house. "I am glad to see you too, but I will let you do the crying."

I would laugh at the idea of Maksim shedding a tear if I wasn't crying so hard. By the time my bawling subsides, we're sitting inside on the couch with me on his lap, and his smile is so bright when I finally lift my head to look him in the face.

Without saying a word, he reaches over to pluck a tissue from the box on the end table and hands it to me. Wiping the wetness off my face, I sit up a little and lean over to toss the tissue in the tiny wastebasket before settling back in the comfort of his embrace.

"I know you will have many questions and I will answer them all, but first…" Cupping my cheek in his hand, he dips his head toward mine, brushing our lips together softly as if he's afraid this is all a dream.

And it feels that way even as his next kiss is longer, firmer as if he's a new lover trying to coax me into letting him in. When he nips at my bottom lip with a soft bite, the invasion of my mouth with his tongue is his sweet victory and my eager submission.

Two years without being touched or kissed by another adult makes me hungry and wishing it wasn't the middle of the fucking day with my daughter taking a nap in her room…because I want to drag him to mine.

He's steady and controlled, holding back as much as I am, both of us putting our hunger and long-suffering need into every wild tangle of our tongues.

My head reels, dizzy with desire as he rips his lips from mine at the sound of Katya's sweet call through the monitor. "Mama?"

Maksim's stunned expression breaks through my haze of arousal, his hands going slack as he stares at the monitor, and I take the opportunity to slip off his lap with a laugh. "You want to meet her, don't you?"

He drags his eyes away from the monitor and back to my face with a nervous smile. "Of course. What did you name her, *lyubimaya*?"

"Ekaterina Odinovna."

He blinks at that, the small intake of breath the only indication he hadn't expected that name choice, before giving a slight nod of acknowledgment. "Beautiful. Does she have a…" He searches for the word in English and snaps his fingers with a proud smirk. "A nickname?"

"I call her Katya." When he opens up his mouth up to say something, I hold up a finger and turn away. "Going to get her before she starts crying."

Katya sits up in bed and reaches out to me with a sleepy smile. "Up!"

Lifting her into my arms, I walk over to her dresser, grab a diaper, and lay her on the floor to change her. The moment that's done, she gets up and takes off with a happy squeal, leaving me to toss the diaper into the bin before chasing after her as usual.

This time, though, instead of hiding under the coffee table, she's standing frozen in the living room entryway, staring at Maksim with her thumb in her mouth.

"Hello, Katya." Maksim speaks gently to her, staring at her before pinning me with his gaze and shakes his head, chuckling. "Nobody would have believed she was my child."

"I know. I've thought the same thing many times."

Katya glances between Maksim and me, walks over to where her toys are sitting in the corner, and plops down with a little 'humph' sound.

"She is not impressed with me," he teases as I walk back over to the couch and sit beside him, his eyes dropping to my neck and darkening while staring at my neck. "Why do you still wear the choker all this time? I called my man to remove it for you on the way to the airport, once I realized I failed to do it myself."

"I...I told him not to." Lifting my hand to touch it, I shrug at him because after this long, I don't even notice it's there unless I'm looking in a mirror. "When you first put it on me, I hated it, but by the time you sent me away, it was just...a part of me. Of our relationship. And all I would have left being separated from you."

Placing a hand on my knee, I can tell it's hard

for him to keep his hands off me other than innocently — especially after that confession — and appreciate his restraint. "You don't need to wear it anymore, *malyshka*. Turn around and let me remove it."

"Why? Do you want it back?"

"No, not at all. It is yours, but my wife is dead. You are not mine any longer."

The idea he doesn't want me, because that's the only reason he says that, causes tears to well in my eyes, my sudden misery mirroring a second later on his face as I whisper, "You don't want me? You didn't come here to...to be together?"

His emotions flash in eyes, voice quiet and fierce as he cups both sides of my face in his hands. "I will always want you, Ramona. I love you and always have. But there are things you must know and then you will make a decision. I will not make it for you, not like before because the whole purpose of getting you away from that life was to make sure you were able to have choices."

"I know." Swallowing, and unable to handle all the emotions in his eyes along with the ones his heartfelt declaration of love make me feel, I sigh and look over at Katya. "Can we talk about all this later, once she's in bed for the night?"

"I think that would be better, yes."

"Good." Touching his hand for a brief second,

I close my eyes and softly ask, "Are you hungry? I can make you something."

"I am starving. The food on the plane wouldn't fill a child, let alone a man that likes to eat as much as I do."

"Okay. I'll make you some lunch."

Laughing, I stand up to walk out and feel his heated gaze burning into my back until I'm out of his sight.

The reprieve won't last long, but it's enough to get me until later this evening, where I have a feeling he'll tell me all the things I want to know... as well as the ones I don't.

10

RAMONA

ONCE KATYA's asleep in her bed, I return to the living room, Maksim tugging me down as I approach the couch, and adjusts my body so I'm straddling his lap facing him.

"Now we talk." Putting his arms loosely around my waist, he smiles sadly. "I thought of where to begin, but decided to ask you what you want to know."

Probably better that way, so I start off with an innocent question. "Okay. How did you know where to find me?"

"I had a copy of all the information. It was easy to do a background check and find you bought this house. A smart move, *malyshka*; I like it."

"Me too."

When I simply stare at him, wanting so many answers but afraid to ask the questions, he brushes a soft kiss on my lips and says, "Take your time, *lyubimaya*, for I am not leaving until you want me to."

"Just tell me everything." I force the words past the tickle of anxiety in my throat, giving him permission to say everything he needs to say without me hiding behind the safety of the unknown. I have been ignorant of what's gone on long enough. "Start with how you knew I needed to leave…"

He grimaces yet his eyes never leave mine as he begins, switching to Russian. "Your father's business was powerful and made a lot of money for many people. He kept his hands clean but it wasn't because he wasn't involved — he got others to do his dirty work for him. Fear ruled. There were others out there stronger than him, though, and they were getting angry at him coming into their territory and slowly taking over. And now he put many people at risk, wouldn't listen to anyone who told him he was going too far."

"You?"

"I tried to tell him. I knew something would go down, especially when he attempted to deal with someone he had angered, and chose to do something about it. And so, in order to save you, I made a deal with those who weren't in your father's pockets and wanted to catch him and those he worked with."

I suck in a breath at realizing he narced in exchange for his life and mine. "So…papa is dead?"

His expression softens, a little guilt in his eyes but no sign of regret. "Yes, but I had nothing to do with that. Those your father wanted to deal with showed up earlier than anticipated and killed him, probably as they planned all along."

"And my mama?"

"I don't know, *malyshka*. She is alive and that is all I know."

Of course, she thinks him dead along with me and I try not to let the pain of never seeing my mama again take over by going back to talking about him. "You weren't in the building?"

"No. But that was part of the deal made before I gave them enough information to hang many people once they were found and arrested. Death was the only way out for both of us, Ramona. Your father had many enemies, but also allies who may have come after us, especially if I didn't step into his shoes upon his death as expected."

I believe him, but tears slide down my cheeks at hearing he's been safe all this time and not here with me. "Why didn't you come to me until now, then? Where have you been?"

"I wasn't free. I had evidence, I needed protection too. I'm not able to give too many details about that, but trust me, I came to you as soon as I could."

"I do. And I'm glad you were kept safe too." We both smile at each other again, and I know tomorrow my face will hurt from all this joy today after so long of having so little. "So what is your name? And are these real, our names? Official?"

"Your papers were real, legitimate, but it is hard to think of you as anything other than as I have known you our whole lives." When I stare at him expectantly, he laughs and says, "I am now known as Anton Leskov."

"I like it. I have gotten used to being referred to as Veronika, but it was a fight to remember to respond and not correct others."

"Same for me as well. But, we are far from Russia so we may call each other whatever we wish in private."

Unsure of what to say to that, or where all this leaves us, silence falls between us. And for a time, I snuggle in his arms with him rubbing my back and occasionally kissing my lips with such tenderness I never want it to end.

Finally, he sighs as if tortured and whispers, "There is something you need to know. Something your father confided in me after our return following the wedding, and I kept from you because there was nothing to be done about it at the time."

Not even lifting my head, thinking it's

something he probably thinks is important but isn't, I snuggle closer to him because I'm sleepy and thinking about asking him to take me to bed. "What is it?"

"I was wrong about him, *malyshka*. He came after you."

I never knew how someone's 'heart-stopping' worked, but mine does, as does my breathing. I can't respond, frozen in a whirl of emotions.

Maksim grabs my arms and makes it so he's staring me in the face with an anxiety-ridden expression. "Did you hear me?"

"You said Owen came to Russia." My response is wooden, disbelieving. "That's not possible. He—he would've come to me."

"He tried. You remember that day in your father's warehouse?" At my nod, he reaches up and strokes the choker, just as he did that day. "That beautiful mirror you admired so much hid a room where he could see you, but we couldn't see him or hear him. He was a few feet away from us and your father made sure he didn't interfere with the wedding by keeping him locked in there."

I don't know how to react or what to feel. Horror, mostly, at knowing my father did such a thing to Owen, but it's been so long. My feelings are jumbled, a tangle of relief and sadness mixing with all the confusion about how I felt about Owen.

He frowns when the only response I make is,

"And you didn't know he was there? You didn't want him near me either, you admitted as much."

"No. I said I knew no good would come of it, but never would I have condoned your father locking up anyone as he did. He kept me extra busy in the weeks leading up to the wedding, both with you and with business outside the warehouse. This was typical of your father — he trusted me the most with more sensitive information and tasks — so it wasn't suspicious to me. If I had noticed, I would have freed him and brought him to you to see what he wanted."

"Okay."

"Okay?" He scowls now, brows furrowed as if he can't figure out why the hell I'm not more excited. "You spent every day leading up to the wedding watching for him, waiting. Fuck, I know you spent our whole wedding day hoping he would walk through that door. You gave birth to his child. Do you not wish to know why he came to Russia?"

Do I? It seems like such a long time ago now. Two and a half years since we saw each other last. And…"I don't know. He might have moved on, be married by now, maybe even have a family with someone else. He didn't love me, Maksim, and maybe even believes I'm dead just like everybody else does."

"The last is likely, but everything else? You won't know unless you go to him, *malyshka*, especially because of Katya. If nothing else, he deserves to know her and she needs her Papa in her life."

He makes sense, of course, he does. Katya does deserve to know her father. But Owen also slept with me and didn't even say goodbye. Why come to Russia when he couldn't even bother to tell me to my face that he was sending me back home? Thinking about his rejection stings and makes my heart ache as it thaws from the shock, and right now I just want to make it go away.

I want to feel, but not like this, and when Maksim releases his hold on me, I snuggle close again with a sniffle. "I'll think about it tomorrow. But, right now, I want to go to bed."

He kisses the top of my head, hugging me close before letting go again. "It's been a long day and you need your rest. I'll see you in the morning."

"No." Slipping off his lap, I hold out my hand toward him. "I want you to come with me. I've spent two years alone, Maksim. At least, give me tonight, no matter what tomorrow brings, because I missed you."

For a moment, as he watches me with guarded eyes, I fear he will turn me down. But then, his whole manner changes as he stands, the desire from earlier back in his eyes and burning bright with promise.

I lead him to my room and shut the door

behind us, but that's where he takes over, allowing me to feel nothing except loved for the first time in too long.

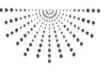

11

OWEN

"Owen?"

Another date, another disappointment.

The sadness in Joy's voice gives that away before I drag my gaze from the TV screen to her face, watching her struggle to hold back her tears. Pressing off on the remote, I place it on the table and open my arms, her own wrapping around my neck two seconds later as she buries her face and cries.

Tonight is the second time this month, following last month with way more, and part of me wants to ask her why she continues to torture herself, but I know why. Most days, she puts on a brave face, pretending she doesn't care about having kids even after her words to me two years ago, but then she breaks like this.

I want to ease her pain, but I don't know how when I can't even alleviate my own. She won't consider having a child on her own, even though she can afford to because she wants the whole family package. I hate seeing her like this. She's a great person, she should get what she wants and needs without so much difficulty.

And, not for the first time, I sit here holding her, the thought of offering her the things she wants myself running through my mind. We may not be in love with each other, but we do love each other and have a rock solid friendship. We wouldn't have to fear letting each other down or ripping a child's life apart with divorce because we've loved each other a long time already. It's not passionate love; instead, a steady never wavering companionship. One that's kept me going in my darkest moments.

"Maybe it's not meant to be," she finally whispers through her tears. "Maybe I want something I'm not supposed to have and I should just stop trying."

The defeat in her statement hits me hard in the chest, echoing the thoughts I've had since Ramona's death. I've punished myself for two years — for not managing to get to her sooner mainly — and hated her just a little even though I probably shouldn't with knowing the life her father trapped her in.

Still I wonder, did she know the truth when she married him? Was that the reason for the sadness on her face that day in the warehouse? She had my contact information, so if the child was mine, why hadn't she called me when she found out? Even if we couldn't have changed our situations, she should have figured out a way to tell me.

And because she didn't, I've been angry for two years, unable to ever have my questions answered.

Unable to let go of the knowledge I would've been a father…or the pain of discovering the opportunity had been stolen from me. Robbed by circumstances, wondering for a while now if, like Joy, a family wasn't in the cards for me either.

But perhaps the problem is us not taking advantage of the chance we have with each other to get what we want, instead of looking for it elsewhere.

"Joy." When she lifts her head to look at me with tear streaked cheeks and sad eyes, I ignore the tightness in my chest at wondering if she'll turn down me offering what I have left to give to her or anyone else. "I know it may not be your ideal, but what about trying with me?"

She doesn't get it immediately, blinking and her lips moving as if she's mouthing the words to understand them, and finally her eyes flare as she sucks in a sharp breath. "You mean…have a family with you?"

"Yes."

"Oh." She lifts a shaky hand and covers her mouth with it as she whispers, "Are you sure?"

"You know I wouldn't ask if I wasn't."

Her enthusiastic reply comes with a kiss and a lot of tears, but at least, they're happy ones this time around.

Simone sits next to me on the couch and hands me a beer, tipping hers a fraction toward where Joy plays blocks with Elijah on the floor. "So…you and Joy?"

"Are we that obvious?"

"You two arrived hand-in-hand, something I've never seen before today…so yes." She sips her beer and raises her brow. "What changed? When?"

"Yesterday. And life did. Both of us wanting a family and not finding it with anyone else."

She places her hand over mine with a smile. "I understand. And after twenty years, who better to parent with than a friend you can trust?"

No need for me to respond, so I don't. She knows how hard what happened hit me and struggled herself during and after returning from the summer course in Russia, feeling responsible for not being able to make contact with Ramona sooner.

Not her fault or anyone else, but it took a while to convince her of that, especially after confronting me about the pregnancy upon arriving at the same conclusion I had. And she cried for me, saying if only she had gone sooner, but we both knew it may not have made a difference in the long run.

"I'm happy for you," she says, pressing my hand in comfort before letting go with a wink. "Now I can worry less about you, which will please Isaac."

Smirking at how much Simone's caring about me bugs Isaac years later, I return her wink with a laugh.

"Thank you. Things should get exciting — and perhaps a bit terrifying — moving forward."

"Ah yeah. Parenthood will do that to you. And speaking of…" She presses a hand against her stomach as her face lights up with delight. "Baby number three for me."

"Going for a football team?"

"No." Her grin turns cheeky. "Just a baseball one, maybe. Malik will be entering kindergarten by the time this one is born, and Elijah…god, he's already almost three. I would love a little girl."

"Let's hope when you do that she looks like you, hm? Those boys resemble him to the point I'm convinced they're mini-dictators in the making."

"Shut up."

Playfully slapping my shoulder with the back of her hand, we both laugh and when Joy glances up, the affectionate look she aims my way would've convinced me I made the right decision if I wasn't certain already.

I am, and for the first time in two years, I'm not paralyzed by fear of what might happen if I take a risk.

~

"Are you coming home soon?"

God, I always thought that question would bug the shit out of me and feel like nagging, but coming from Joy it doesn't. Two weeks as an official couple and there's just something right about it in a way I hadn't expected and can't explain. "About an hour. I need to finish up here and make sure this new manager has everything under control, all right?"

"I trained him so of course he does." She snickers when I sigh and says, "I'm sorry. It's just…time, so be prepared to get naked the moment you walk in."

"Looking forward to it."

She hangs up with a quick 'bye,' and the new manager, Phil, laughs as he stands up. "Wives, huh? Mine can't wait for me to get home either."

Joy wants to keep our personal relationship out of work, a decision we both agree is best, so I just grin and say, "Yeah. She's pretty great."

A soft, forceful gasp sounds from the direction of the doorway and the only thing I catch a glimpse of is the back of a woman wearing a long black skirt and matching heels as she hurries away.

Phil distracts me from my curiosity at what she might've wanted with another chuckle. "Owen, man, if you want to go, I've got this. Joy trained me to rather exacting standards, on top of the ones I already had from managing other restaurants back in Seattle."

"I'm sure she did, but this is the first time since we opened that someone other than Joy or I will be in charge as a general manager."

"I get it, but no need to worry. I didn't come highly recommended for nothing."

"You're right. I wouldn't have hired you otherwise." Standing up, I grab my suit jacket and put it on, walking around the desk while extending my hand for him to shake. "It's all yours, and just remember, I'm not afraid to fire you."

A minute later, I stop inside the doors leading outside, taking my phone from my pocket to text Joy. "*Leaving now, be ready for me.*"

"*Already am. Hurry.*"

Pushing open the door, I step outside into the approaching darkness of the evening and head toward the car waiting for me, distracted with thoughts of what-ifs in case Joy gets pregnant sooner rather than later.

But then, the sound of a woman softly crying in the direction I just came from lands my attention, and right as I'm about to turn around to see if she needs help, the quiet, comforting tone of a man...speaking rapidly in Russian.

Fuck. No. Fuck no!

Pivoting, they don't see me approaching as they stand facing away, the man's arm around the woman wearing the black skirt.

They both jump at the sound of my voice.

"I don't know what you're doing out here or why you almost came into my office only to rush out," I say in Russian, anger coursing through me at feeling like they were up to no good for some reason. "But you need to leave, now."

They both turn at the same time, but my focus is on the woman, and at the sight of her tear streaked and all too familiar face, my whole body inside and out goes cold.

"Hello, O...Owen," she whispers, staring at me, her eyes wide and filled with pain.

What the fuck does she have to be hurt about? Isn't she supposed to be fucking dead?

"Chandler," comes the simple greeting from the man beside her before I can process the fact of who stands before me, his smile not quite reaching his eyes when I look over at him.

Aristov.

No thinking is necessary because, in an instant, I know what happened two years ago, the answers to all my questions staring at me in the fucking face.

And I react because I'm pissed for thinking her

dead all this time, for finally moving on only for her to pop up in my life like nothing happened.

My fist connects with Aristov's face before he knows what has hit him, Ramona screaming as he stumbles back with a stunned expression, and I don't even look at her or say another word before striding back toward my car.

12

RAMONA

"STOP!" He ignores me and keeps walking, so I scream louder. "Fucking stop, damn you."

"Go, *lyubimaya*." Maksim speaks from behind me with a chuckle. "We surprised him, is all, but don't let him leave without having your say."

"He punched you!" Stepping forward, I lift a hand to the swiftly bruising area of his face. "Are you all right?"

"I am fine. He hits like a pussy." He winks at that because we both know it hurts like hell. "Go to him. I will wait in the car with Katya and the babysitter."

I don't see the point. I heard him agree with that man about having a wife, and even though I intended to tell him about Katya no matter what, I hadn't wanted him to see my reaction to hearing he married.

Irrational, but I stupidly let a little hope creep in as we traveled here, wondering if being a family with him was possible. But, now I know, and I can't let him walk away without meeting his daughter.

Kissing Maksim on the cheek, he turns away to get in the car and I take off at what counts as running in heels, shouting in Russian at Owen's retreating form. "I swear, if you don't stop right now, I will slash your fucking tires the next time I see your car!"

He stops by his car and opens the door, not acknowledging me at all, yet merely stands there, waiting.

By the time I reach him, I'm out of breath, and he turns around slow enough fear snakes through me at what I'll see on his face.

Coldness. His eyes, his expression, and his voice when he speaks are all colder than winter in northern Russia. "Tell me how the fuck a dead woman is chasing me down a sidewalk."

"Ramona isn't standing in front of you. She is dead." Straightforward and accurate, and his eyes narrow even more as he glares at me. "Here, I am Veronika, and he…he is Anton."

"Good for both of you. I hope you're happy together here in America." I don't miss his sarcasm as he glances at his phone and then glares at me again. "If you don't mind, I need to get home. I have more important things to do than give a shit about someone who didn't give two shits about me."

"Fuck you," I snap, taking a step toward him and stabbing him in the chest with my index finger. "You think coming here was easy for me after how you sent me away? I didn't have to. I could have been happy with him arriving and never talked to you again."

Liar, liar...

He snatches my hand, gripping it tight as he hisses right back at me, eyes blazing with fire now. "No, fuck you. How the hell did you think I would feel after believing you dead for two years? You and my child, the one you didn't even tell me you were pregnant with, fucking murdered—"

"What?" Jerking my head back, my mind reels. "How did you know—"

"On your local news. Twenty-two weeks, Ramona. I can fucking add, that's how."

"Oh my god..." No wonder he's so angry, lashing out in his hurt. "I...I'm so sorry. I wanted to tell you but it's complicated. That's why I came so we could talk."

"What is there to talk about?"

Tears well in my ears and pent up emotions tickle my throat as I stare into his eyes, letting him see how sorry I am. "The fact nobody murdered me, Owen, which means over nineteen months ago, in hiding and all alone, I went to the hospital and gave birth to a little girl who needs her father."

He lets go of my hand like it's on fire — as if

he hadn't considered that as possibility — all the color draining from his face as he takes a step back, and his voice cracking with emotion when he finally asks, "We have a daughter?"

"Yes."

"And you—" He cuts off as his phone buzzes in his hand, shoving a hand through his hair after reading whatever is on the screen. A message from his wife I'll bet, especially when he looks at me again and frowns. "Do you know where I live?"

"Yes, I have your address. I just came here first because I figured you were working."

"Are you able to come there tomorrow morning at eleven?" When I nod, he says, "Good. I will see you then."

"Okay."

He gets into the car without another word and shuts the door, leaving me walking back to the car — Maksim, despite what he said, is leaning against it as he waits for me — while wondering how tomorrow will go.

Either way, I'm ready to face everything, and move on with my newfound freedom.

"ARE YOU OKAY, *LYUBIMAYA*?"

"No."

Katya naps in my arms as we sit in the living room inside Owen's house waiting for him to come in. A housekeeper had greeted us at the door and informed us he was busy but would be with us shortly.

That was half an hour ago.

"Maybe we should leave," I tell him with a shrug, trying to keep calm even though I feel like crying. "We've waited long enough."

Maksim shakes his head and turns toward me, holding out his hands. "Give Katya to me and go find him, *malyshka*. Then, give him a piece of your mind, hm?"

"I can't just walk around."

"Yes, you can, or I will do it. And if I do, he will be paid back for last night and more."

"Violence won't solve anything."

He grins at that, gently pulling Katya out of my arms and into his, and shakes his head. "I would never say it is the solution to anything. Now, go. We will be all right."

Reluctant but resigned, I walk out of the room and stop in the hallway, wondering which direction I should go. I never saw much of the house before and after having thought how big it looked from the outside earlier, now I'm sure I will get lost inside here without guidance on where to go.

Lucky for me, when I walk into the kitchen, a man wearing a chef's hat looks up at me and smiles. "You are lost, aren't you?"

"Da." When he frowns at me, I blush at having

answered him in Russian and switch to English. "Yes. I need to speak with Owen and it seems he's forgotten about me waiting. It's urgent."

Not true. However, if there is one thing I've learned, it's that telling a person it's urgent or an emergency here will get you what you want more often than not. Doesn't always work, but the man smiles at me and points straight in the air with his knife.

"His office is up the steps you passed to get here, to the left, and straight until the end of the hallway. But I didn't tell you this."

"Of course. Thank you."

It takes less than two minutes with his directions, and as I approach the door, I hear rather than see Owen speaking and pause so I don't interrupt. "Are you sure?"

A choked response from an obviously emotional Joy surprises me. "Of course, I am. Don't be a fool, Owen. This changes everything."

"I don't break my promises, Joy, and—"

"You're not. I am breaking it for you. This is everything you want and hoped for. Now you should go downstairs and figure out what happened and where to go from here."

Now is the time to announce my presence before they both walk out and find me standing here. After a deep breath, I walk the few feet to the door and knock on the frame, taking a few steps into the room as both Joy and Owen turn to see who it is from where they stand next to a window.

Joy is the first to move, walking toward me with a kind smile and her hands clasped in front of her, which is at odds with her eyes red from crying. She stops in front of me and says, "I will leave you two alone. Is she downstairs?"

"Yes, Maksim is with her."

Her eyebrows rise at that. "The man you married?"

"He is, but we aren't any longer."

"Ah, well, death will do that." She grins when I can't help except laugh at her putting it that way and then she puts her hand on my shoulder to squeeze it. "I'm glad you are well. You two come downstairs once you aren't angry enough to strangle each other anymore."

Leaving, she shuts the door softly behind her, and Owen gestures with one hand toward the chair across from his desk.

After I've taken a seat, he returns to leaning on the windowsill while looking out, and just when I think he's intent on torturing me with silence, he lets out a long and heavy sigh. "Why did you come into the restaurant last night, only to run out without saying anything?"

Straight to embarrassment on my end because the way I feel makes me...well, feel out of line, especially, after all, this time has passed. Great. "I overheard you talking about how great wives are with that man. Are you married?"

"No. Your arrival put an end to any plans I was making, however."

Plans for what? I don't understand…Oh. Oh! Suddenly, the conversation I heard between Joy and Owen makes sense, and my whole face burns at realizing she had just ended things between them before I entered.

"I'm sorry. The last thing I wanted was to ruin things for you. I can go—"

"You will over my dead body." Cursing, he circles around to face me, rubbing a hand down his face before frowning. "I shouldn't have said that."

"Why not?" For some reason, I can't hold back the tickle in my throat and I cover my mouth as a little giggle escapes. "Technically, we're both dead, aren't we?"

His mouth flattens in a grim line even as his eyes light up in a way I remember all too well. "This isn't fucking funny."

That only turns the giggles into full blown laughter and I don't know why I'm laughing. Doesn't matter though because soon, my mirth evolves into sobs, both my hands covering my face in an attempt to stifle them or hide them. I don't know anymore.

Feeling his arms sliding around my waist as he pulls me up from the chair, I only move enough to wrap mine around his neck, and then he sits down with me in his lap. And I wait for him to talk, to say everything I've feared and desired, but he doesn't.

He just holds me until the tears eventually slow to a stop, keeping me close to him with a tight embrace as he says, "Tell me everything."

And I do, starting from the time he sent me home and including everything Maksim said to me because I've got nothing left to lose.

13

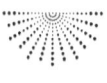

OWEN

THE MOMENT RAMONA made it clear we did have a child together last night, I knew telling Joy would result in her ending any personal relationship between us, and she wouldn't give me a say in the decision.

I understand her choice, but she's hurting and that bothers me. Hurting someone is the last thing I ever want to do, even if it's not intentional. She's putting on a brave face for me and in front of Ramona this morning; however, her crying last night said it all. I comforted her earlier, tried to tell her nothing had to change, all while attempting to work up the nerve to head downstairs and meet my child.

Terrified. Not manly to admit that, but I am terrified and unsure of what to do.

Fucking ridiculous. I always know what to do, except this whole situation is beyond belief, even though I'm living through it. And the story

Ramona's just finished telling me makes it worse because I've been angry at a woman I knew truly had no choice all along.

She didn't tell me because she feared for my life, her own, and that of our child. How can I fucking be pissed at that even if I missed out on the first eighteen months?

I don't get to spend time figuring this out or step back and say, 'let me wrap my head around the fact you're alive and we have a child together' to her. We're in an unusual predicament, leaving me out of my element and reluctant to trust in it. The problem is, I have to. This is real.

This is fucking authentic and downstairs is a little girl. My daughter. And I'm not willing to miss another moment of her life, not as long as I'm alive and have a say in it.

Ramona dries her eyes, waiting for me to say something after everything she's just told me, including that she knew her father kept me locked up until after the wedding.

She said sorry, her whole face miserable as if that were her fault. Like any of this is. If anything, I want to punch Aristov again for touching her, even if she's spent the whole time defending him with every breath. Because of her defense.

He knew what her father was like and kept her in the dark even with his plan to roll over on the family all along. He claimed forcing her into submission was to protect her, to make sure she kept her head down, even more so after he knew she was pregnant with my child. I see the love for him in her eyes and hear it in her voice; if I let her, she'll go with him and be happy in her own mind.

But it would be wrong because she didn't give in willingly; she merely believes she did. Being told to keep silent or risk having others hurt or killed is blackmail, a tactic to get her to behave even if nothing would happen in truth. She'll learn, though — you can't give anything willingly when you're backed into a corner. It's survival, it's keeping yourself alive while hoping for something better, but between a rock and a hard place is never an actual choice.

Nevertheless, in the end, he got her away and saved her and the baby, and while I might've gotten away with punching him once, I doubt she would be happy if I did it again. Lucky him.

I want to make her stay, yet she's had enough men in her life telling her what to do. If we do that, it will because she wants it as much as I do, not because she has no option. Despite that, my lot in life hasn't happened by chance and if I can't demand, I will phrase the demand as a strong suggestive statement, perhaps even a question.

Because although she hadn't said it straight, she ran out of my restaurant while upset at thinking I had married. She came here with hopes and I need to show her they can turn into something concrete.

Swiping at the tear on her cheek, I finally come to a plan I can live with, and smile at her for the first time since seeing her last night. "I'm sorry you had to go through that, that you've lost your home and family. But I'm glad it's over and you are both safe."

"Me too."

"We have a lot more to discuss." When she nods in agreement, I ask the question I should've asked before now. "Tell me our daughter's name."

She lowers her gaze, pulling her lip into her mouth and biting it as her face flushes, and then murmurs, "Ekaterina Odinovna. I call her Katya."

"Beautiful." Cupping her face in my hand, I lift her chin so my mouth can cover hers in a sweet kiss meant to show her how much I love the name she chose. Also, to thank her for the strength and bravery it must have taken to have our child, all alone and thinking she would never see the father of her child again.

And because I need to say it, even if she doesn't care about hearing it, I pull back and whisper against her lips, "I'm sorry for sending you away without saying goodbye. You deserved better. You were entitled to consideration and respect, and you should've received it even though I was angry and distrustful."

"Thank you." Her eyes fill with renewed tears, her lips trembling even as she shakes her head. "You might disagree, but I think it best that everything went this way. My papa was more dangerous than I knew. I loved him, and I miss him, but part of me is happy he can't hurt me or others for his own gain anymore."

Maybe some things might have been different, but she's right. What he might've done if she hadn't returned home doesn't bear consideration. "I understand. He had a lot of power and knew how to wield it. Would have to, especially to have enough pull with the government to get a man banned from Russia so he won't return and convince your daughter to leave."

"You were?" At my nod, she winces and shakes her head. "It's true, isn't it? Maksim said he never intended to let us marry."

"I know. He told me everything, including how he let you believe we were to marry for his own selfish reasons, before locking me up. Turns out the only thing he ever told the truth about what helping my father leave — but I believe your father helped not because they were friends, but because it gave him all the control with my father out."

A tear slips down her cheek, but she wipes at it and sits up in my arms, squaring her shoulders and lifting her chin in defiance. "I will never understand how Papa could be callous enough to treat me that way. I won't be like that to Katya, and neither will anyone else."

"Is that a warning?" She blushes, making me

grin as I move my hands to her waist, lifting her off my lap and onto her feet. Rising to my own, I assure her, "Children aren't tools to be used by their parents for their own gain. I promise you'll never have to worry about that with me. Plus, it's not smart to piss off or fuck with a woman who threatens to slash your tires."

Face flaming, she laughs and places her hand on my arm. "I'm not worried."

I like the fact she doesn't apologize for her threat. "Good. Now, before we head downstairs and I have my heart stolen forever by a little girl, tell me you will stay."

"Stay? As in, here with you?"

"Yes."

"Because of Katya? There is no need. I can get a place of my own, somewhere close so you can see her whenever you want."

Smiling, I take her hands in mine and lace our fingers together, leaning in until I can almost cover her lips with mine if I want. "Let me rephrase. I want you to stay — both of you. Katya, because I have missed out on so much already, and you, because we share a child and should get to know one another better."

She lowers her eyes, staring down at the floor for a few seconds, and then looks up at me with an amused smirk. "If I don't agree, will you lock me up in that room again?"

"I might."

I'm teasing, which I know she realizes because the smile she withholds reaches her widening eyes anyway, and she plays along with a demure, "Well, I guess I can't say no then, can I?"

"Guess not." Releasing one of her hands, I motion toward the door. "Shall we?"

"Go ahead. I had to ask for directions, but I'm not telling you who gave them to me."

"Fine with me." Leading her out of the room, I guide her back downstairs and toward the living room, stopping outside the door to take a calming breath. "It's a big house. You'll find your own way before long."

She doesn't say anything, merely stepping around me and walking through the door, where I hear the most beautiful sound in the world.

My daughter's giggle followed by an excited scream. "Mama!"

I'm in love before even entering the room, discovering a little blonde head buried in the crook of Ramona's neck and tiny arms wrapped around her neck.

As I halt just inside the door, all my focus on those two, Ramona turns to me and walks closer, tears gleaming in her eyes as she says, "Katya. Mama wants you to meet someone."

Katya slowly lifts her head, thumb in her mouth and her round, green eyes that are so much like my own filled with curiosity, not doing anything except blinking as she stares at me.

Which is fine with me, because I can't stop looking at her either.

Ramona gets her attention and points at herself. "Mama." Then, she points at me and says, "Papa. This is your papa."

Katya, who looks back and forth between her mother and me for a second in confusion, takes her thumb out of her mouth and promptly bursts into tears.

I get it, because if I were the type of man to cry, I would join in from the simple overabundance of emotions flowing through me right now, too.

14

OWEN

LATER IN THE EVENING, while Ramona is putting Katya to sleep for the night — in a toddler bed I paid extra to have rush delivered from a local store after lunch — I head to my office to make a phone call.

Simone picks up on the second ring with a smile evident in her voice. "Hey, Owen. You have perfect timing, I just put the boys to bed."

"Well, I love hearing how much I have you all to myself, as always."

She laughs just as I knew she would and I can practically hear her rolling her eyes at me. "You're shameless."

"I know. Are you sitting down?"

"No. Should I be? Wait." The sound of her sigh as she sits down — probably one of the few times a day she gets to thanks to those boys of hers — is loud, and after a few seconds she says, "Okay,

I know if you want me to sit down it's serious, so what is it?"

"This is going to sound crazy but I promise, I'm not kidding."

"All right. Tell me, you're making me nervous, especially since I thought I could stop worrying about you."

"You can. See, last night, I found out Ramona is alive. Well, sort of."

"What? Sort of, as in she's a zombie? Are you drunk?"

No." Chuckling, I grip the phone tighter in my hand. "She's here and has been in hiding for two years, Simone. Under a different name, but alive."

She sucks in a sharp breath. "What…Owen. Are you serious?"

"Yes. And I called you because I know you were as messed up about this as I was. But you weren't too late. Her death was all a set up by her husband to take down her father." It's the simplified version but that's all she needs to know at this point.

"Oh…wow." She sniffles. "I don't know what to say."

Because I can't resist shocking her, I suggest with blatant cheer, "How about telling me you'll come over tomorrow and meet my daughter."

Her squeal of shock-slash-excitement is louder this time, and after I explain, she bawls. Which explains why Isaac takes the phone and asks me what I fucking said to upset his wife, requiring me to repeat myself all over again.

Then, after getting over his own shock, he promises they'll come over tomorrow because he's got some questions of his own for Ramona and Maksim, and immediately hangs up on me.

Laughing, I slip the phone into my pocket and head back downstairs, only to stop upon entering the living room at the sight of Maksim and Joy sitting extremely close to each other on the couch with drinks in hand.

Joy raises both her eyebrows at me as if daring me to say anything, but even if I want to punch Maksim in his face, what they both do is none of my business. I'll just warn her to be careful later; however, I haven't missed the heated looks between them since coming downstairs with Ramona earlier.

Shrugging, I walk over to the bar and pour myself a drink, then turn to both of them and say, "We need to talk about tomorrow."

"Hi."

Ramona stands in the doorway of my bedroom, her eyes darting around as she examines the interior, yet doesn't step inside.

"Hey." Sitting up against the headboard, I

mute the TV and pat the bed beside me. "I figured you were in bed already."

"I tried. Couldn't sleep."

"Well, come in, shut the door, and have a seat." Facing the TV again, I turn the volume back on, making it her decision. "Or not. Your choice."

Difficult as it is to keep my focus on the screen instead of her, it pays off as she does exactly as I suggested, climbing onto the bed to sit next to me after slowly crossing the room. And for a little while, we sit next to each other in silence, until whatever the hell this crap is we're watching rolls the credits.

She turns toward me, and once I shut off the TV and return the favor, she grimaces. "This is strange."

"What is?"

"This. Sitting on a bed, watching television, not touching. With you. Where is the man who took advantage of a storm to get into my bed? He would have gotten me into his bed and made me get naked by now."

"A lot has changed in two years."

"Ah, yes, such as your relationship with Joy?"

"I meant for both of us, but yes." She crosses her arms, waiting, and while I knew this moment would come, I hadn't expected it would be so hard to find the words to explain without invading Joy's privacy. "After I returned from Russia, as I tried to figure out where to go from there, we began scene-ing together again. No sex. That came a bit later. But it wasn't serious until recently."

"And then I rose from the dead." She tilts her head to the side, studying me for an instant, and then lifts her hands in a confused shrug. "You were together, why does she not fight for you? She just hands you over to me like your relationship was nothing."

"We care deeply for one another, but Joy wants a relationship with a man who doesn't have children with anyone else." When her eyebrows raise in surprise and she opens her mouth, I stop her with a shake of my head and holding up my hand. "We are friends. Good friends, who were going to give each other a family because neither of us had it, and knew we would be good at it together. The moment she knew were you alive as well as our child, she ended it. And I understand."

"But why? You do not care for me as you do her."

"That's not really true. Because the day I thought you dead, it hurt way more than I expected it would." Reaching between us, I cover her hand with mine and smile. "I told myself it was because I was trying to save you, but I had hopes of what might happen if you wanted to leave Aristov. I tried not to because there was a chance you were happy with him since he was your friend, but they were the same hopes I know you had when you walked into my restaurant last night."

"I see."

Ignoring the tears gathering in her eyes, I clasp my hand around hers instead of merely covering it. "Joy knew this all along. Yes, she is hurt, and that's because she aches for the same thing — a husband and children of her own. However she is happy for me —for us — that you are alive and I have a chance to build a life with you and Katya."

"Would you have been happy with her if I hadn't come back? If I had truly died?"

"Happiness with Joy would've been what we made it, and we would've found something that worked for us. Similar to what you said you had with Aristov when you were married to him."

Her shoulders shake, tears sliding down her eyes as she nods her understanding and then asks softly, "You want me? And Katya. Here, for good?"

"Nothing would make me happier. And you ask why I don't just tell you to get naked. Make no mistake, I will gladly require you to do many things when you belong to me. But the first choice? To choose me and become a family? You must want that willingly, accept everything it means on your own."

She scoots closer until our legs touch, where I can reach out and grab her if I want, our faces less than half a foot apart. "And if I say yes, that I choose you? What am I accepting?"

One of my hands finds a new home on her waist while the other slides up her arm to cup the back of her neck, and she places her hands against my chest. "If you want the same thing I do, then that's what you will get the moment you say yes. And it's forever, Ramona. There is no giving up, there is no separating, no divorce. We have our whole lives to love each other and to keep finding ways to love each other every day because anything less is unacceptable. Is that clear?"

"It is." When her gaze drops to my lips, she licks her own and then her next question is... excited. "Does that mean if I try to leave, you'll lock me up in that room?"

"That's the second time you've brought it up, so yeah, if you want it bad enough, I'll give it to you."

"You will only give it to me."

The flash of temper in her eyes makes me grin. "I can see your mouth still hasn't learned its most important lesson."

"I'm sure you will make it so, or at least try."

Pressing my lips to hers to caress more than kiss them, I pull back when she tries to deepen it. "When you agree, I will. So answer me. Are you mine?"

She sighs, her hands gripping my shirt as she

clings to me, need dripping from every word. "Yes. I choose you, O."

"Already earning a spanking, pet?"

"Yes, sir," she whispers in my ear with a happy laugh. "I don't know why I liked it, but I did, and I want you to do it again."

"Right this second?" Dragging her toward me until she's straddling my lap, I nip at her lip after she nods and say against her mouth, "Looks like it's time to play, pet."

She laughs, wrapping her arms and legs to cling to me as I leave the bed, and take her to the room where we'll spend the rest of our lives fulfilling each other's fantasies.

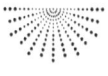

15

RAMONA

HE LEAVES the room after depositing me in the center of it, a naughty glint in his eyes matching the grin on his face as he promises he'll be right back, and a warning to get ready for when he returns.

Undressing, I place my clothes in a neat pile on the floor near the end of the bed and sink to my knees after returning to where he left me.

Still reeling from him saying he wants me and Katya to stay forever, that he intends to be a family with us, it's all I can think about as I wait for him in the position he requires. Hard for me to believe after these two years that he wants to pick up where we left off and of course, this isn't really where we left it because now we share a child.

A large part of me is excited — yes I had hoped and yes this is everything I could possibly want after everything that has happened — but I'm a little afraid. Not enough to keep me from agreeing to stay, to share his home, and to be his, just…enough I will remain careful with my feelings. I don't want to overwhelm any of us, especially Katya.

And although she cried earlier, by bedtime she had warmed up to him quite a bit, even getting close enough to stand nearby and stare at him. I know she will adjust to all the new changes and that I made the right decision to come here at the sight of the instant love shining in O's eyes when he saw her for the first time.

He will be a great papa to Katya, there is no worry there for me. It is everything else that is new and fragile, built on a hope between both of us because of what we already have, yet will take time to steady. I have to trust this second chance, and our attraction, to lead everything else in the right direction.

When he walks back into the room, I resist the strong urge to lift my gaze from the floor, keeping it lowered even as his bare feet move into my line of vision as he halts in front of me.

"Stand up, pet," he says, offering his hand.

Even while placing my hand on his, I laugh softly and say, "So soon? What is the point of getting me on my knees if you're not going to take advantage of it?"

"Good thing you're already on the way to receiving a spanking." Once I'm on my feet, he tugs me over to the bed and sits down, placing me face down across his lap. Without warning he lands the first slap, following up the unexpected sting with a soft caress, and demanding, "Count."

"One, sir," I sing sweetly, wiggling in his lap, and giggling when he grabs my ass with both his hands.

"Spread your legs."

"Two, sir." The words leave on a gasp after I do as he says and he slaps me between my legs.

He does it repeatedly, waiting each time for me to count, and by the tenth, tears are running down my cheeks at the same time I want him to do it again. Then, he caresses me, running one hand over every inch of me to soothe the places smarting from his smacks, while the fingers on his other hand glide between my legs to play.

Sensitive and already slick from arousal, he slips two fingers inside my pussy and then out, teasing my clit before returning to enter me, heightening the pleasure while denying me the orgasm just out of reach.

Shaking from trying to hold back, I try to thrust toward his hand while begging, "Please."

"Please what, pet?"

"Please, may I come sir? I can't wait!"

He takes his touch away entirely, smacking me on the ass one final time before releasing a dark chuckle. "Sure you can."

Lifting me, he lifts me and places me on his lap, straddling him so we face each other with our bodies close as they can be. His cock is hard against my stomach and as he stares at me with a mischievous grin, I wrap my arms around his neck and give his chin a sweet kiss.

He blinks, his smile softening as his arms tighten around my waist. "What was that for?"

"Because I can and anytime I want, at that." Moving my hands to grip his shoulders, I lift my hips and grind against him, hoping to entice him into giving in. "Not to tell you what to do, sir, but I would like a repeat of the last time I was in this bed with you."

"Everything?" He kisses me sweetly when I nod and then asks with a brilliant smile, "Before I tie you up and have my way with you, I believe we should discuss how many children we will have."

The idea of more babies makes me happy because I definitely don't want Katya to be an only child like me. And the fact he wishes to know makes me giddy with anticipation at having him be there this time. "I will say at least one more."

Pressing a kiss to my shoulder with a hearty laugh, he slips his hand between our bodies and then my legs. "Ten total?"

"*Akh, net!*"

I feel him smile against my shoulder, realizing he's teasing even as he continues teasing me with his wicked fingers and playful words. "No? You want more? That's insane, pet. When would we find time to fuck with more than ten children?"

"At this rate, sir, we won't be having any because you're doing too much talking and not enough engaging in the activity that leads to it."

His head goes back a little as he laughs with such joy before standing with me in his arms and turning to put me flat on my back on the bed. "Listen to you. 'Engaging in the activity that leads to it.' You will have to beg me, pet. To fuck you, that is."

Disentangling our bodies, he pulls away and yanks my body toward the edge of the bed, dropping to crouch between my legs and gripping my thighs while I grip his hair in my hands.

And I do beg as he gets me off with his mouth more than once until I'm screaming, pleading for him to tie me to the bed and fuck me.

It's everything I wanted and more, leaving me sure I made the right decision, and looking forward to having this the rest of my life.

THE SOUND OF CHILDREN RUNNING THROUGH THE house, yelling and howling and laughing, greets me when I walk downstairs the next morning.

All right, it's the early afternoon because after keeping me up late, O apparently let me sleep in while rising for the day himself.

Not recalling him mentioning anyone coming to visit, I walk into the living room as two little boys run past me as they chase a squealing Katya, and find O sitting on one couch alone while a man as big as O and a softly smiling woman sit close to each other on the love-seat.

The woman spots me standing in the doorway first and beams at me as she says, "You're up! The kids didn't wake you, did they?"

O jumps up and walks over, grabbing my hand in his while I shake my head at her, before dragging me over to sit with him and introducing them. "This is Isaac and Simone. Simone is my friend; Isaac is her husband and merely tolerates my existence."

"Nice to meet you," I say to them both with a light laugh at the smirk on Isaac's face at O's comment. "If I had known we were going to have guests, I would have made sure to get up earlier."

"Oh! Don't worry about it. After everything you've been through, you deserve the extra rest. And Katya is adorable — she looks so much like Owen!" She puts a hand on her stomach and throws an adoring look Isaac's way. "We're hoping for a girl this time around and that she looks like me."

Isaac raises one brow. "You don't believe the female version of me would be attractive?"

"Imagine yourself in a dress and you have your answer."

All of us laugh as Isaac scowls and just as I'm

about to ask Simone when she's due, Maksim's shocked voice comes from the doorway.

"You!" By the time I look over, he's stalking toward me and puts a hand on my shoulder while glaring at everybody else. "You were following us in Russia."

Simone nods, her eyes wide and face reddening, and Isaac sits forward with a serious expression right then. "Yeah, didn't Owen tell you we came there after he was banned, to try and see if Ramona was all right? I only saw you the one time in the store."

"Yes," O says with a sigh beside me, shrugging when I look over at him because he hadn't told me that. "I told him you were coming last night, but apparently he was too drunk to recall the conversation we had."

"No," Maksim says, removing his hand from my shoulder and crossing his arms over his chest, nodding at Isaac and Simone. "I remember her from the market, but he followed us more than she did."

"What?" Both O and Simone stare at Isaac while saying this at the same time as if...they didn't know?

He doesn't look at Owen, only at Simone. "What did you think I would do when you were taking your class? I kept an eye on his house and spent time trying to figure out how to approach while he was at work, but she was being watched and I never had the chance."

"I had her *protected*," Maksim hisses although he doesn't move from where he stands. "You think my men didn't see you? The only reason they didn't approach you is because I told them to merely keep an eye on you."

Isaac doesn't flinch as he meets Maksim's angry gaze. "I made sure they did. No need for the anger, I assure you. We wanted her safe as much as you did, if not more."

"You almost jeopardized things with your antics because her father watched us. As for her safety, I'm the one who put my life on the line to get her to safety."

I'm not surprised my father watched us, but I am a little shocked at Maksim's anger considering where we are now. They couldn't have known my Papa kept an eye on us; it's not their fault or mine that we were necessarily oblivious to his plans.

Rising from my seat, I move to stand in front of him and make sure he's looking at me before pleading softly, "Please stop. It doesn't matter now. We are both here and safe, and your protection worked out. They were there to help me if I wanted it."

He lifts a hand to my face, caressing my cheek before dropping his hand with a sigh, the sadness in it matching the grief he's hidden so well until now in his eyes. "It is a choice I made to protect you, *lyubimaya*, but don't forget that I lost my family in this as well. I am happy for you that you will have such loyal protectors here."

"Me too." And because I'll never be able to say it enough, I take his hands in mine and kiss his cheek, whispering, "Thank you. For everything."

I don't know what I expected, but he doesn't say anything else, just tosses a final glaring glance at the others in the room before kissing my cheek, turning around and walking out.

And knowing he is the one who encouraged me to come here to perhaps work things out with O doesn't make my heart hurt any less at realizing the part of him that loved me hoped he would get to keep me.

Nor does it keep me from crying when the sound of the front door closing makes it clear he just made his goodbye without actually saying it.

I am just glad O is there to wrap me in his arms and hold me tightly, my sadness at saying farewell to the life I had colliding with the bittersweet promise of the future with O.

EPILOGUE

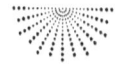

Ramona

THE DAY of our wedding is nothing like my first one, and while I'm excited to marry again, I'm sad because my mother isn't with me this time.

I don't think I will ever get over not having my mama in my life, not as long as she might be alive, and this alone makes me determined to ensure every moment I have is spent with Katya and any other future children.

Six months of living with Owen — I've gotten used to his name now, as he has to calling me Veronika...in polite company, at least — has me looking forward to the day I can tell him we're going to have another baby together. We decided to wait until after we were married to try for another, which has also allowed us to spend this time getting to know each other, as well as figuring out how well we parent together.

This is a lot easier than I thought it might be; Owen is just as protective as Katya as I am, and just as doting. We agree a lot more than we disagree, and even when we do, it's because he doesn't think there's anything wrong with her having a cookie right before dinner. He is wrapped around her little finger and revels in it, so sometimes I will scowl on the outside while melting on the inside at the affection in his eyes for both of us as he hands her the cookie anyway, then whispers promises into my ear for later.

Thinking about the ones he made for this evening before leaving me earlier today until the ceremony makes me grin.

"Oh, I know that smile," Simone remarks with a laugh, putting the finishing touches on my hairstyle for the day. "I wear it often when Isaac is around."

"I am glad to have a friend who understands."

"Same. I think Owen's getting put out by the fact I talk to you more than him now, but I told him he needs to get some more friends too."

"Poor him. He will get over it."

She steps back with a laugh and both of us frown at the sudden knock on the bedroom door. Nobody other than the woman taking care of the children today is supposed to come up here, so hoping nothing is going poorly I call out, "Come in!"

"*Lyubimaya*, you must join me out here."

Delighted at knowing Maksim has come for my wedding — he ended up going back to the house I bought and recently purchased it from me because he wants to live there for good — I stand up and walk over to the door, swinging it open with a cry of happiness. "You surprised me!"

He steps forward with a grin and envelops me in his arms, hugging me tight as always, before pulling back and taking my hand in his. "I need you to come downstairs. I have a gift for you."

"But aren't gifts for after the ceremony—?"

"No. I promise you that you will want it before the wedding. Come with me, hm? It is almost time anyway, correct?"

His insistence makes me suspicious of what is waiting for me downstairs. "Yes, but I'm not ready yet."

"Here." Simone steps up behind me and puts on my veil, then says, "All right, now you're ready."

"Okay. Thank you!"

Maksim tugs on my hand with an impish smile, leading me toward whatever he has waiting, although he walks slower than he normally would so I can keep up with him in my dress and heels.

He doesn't stop until we're standing by the door in the kitchen, which leads to the courtyard and where the wedding is going to be, and that's where he turns to me and takes both my hands in his.

"You are stunning, *malyshka.*"

"Thank you. You look handsome, too, and I'm glad you decided to come."

"Ah, *lyubimaya*, I would never have missed your wedding, no matter how far away I am or for how long."

"Good." I try to look past his shoulder and out the window, but he blocks my view. "What did you do?"

"Nothing. I would like to walk you down the aisle if you will let me? Either way, we will go now."

I want to cry but hold back my tears because I don't want to ruin my makeup. "I would like that and it's a lovely gift."

He grins, hugs me again, and then gestures outside. "Shall we?"

Nodding at him, he opens the door and lets me walk through first, following behind me and shutting the door before offering his arm to me. Looping mine through, he leads us along the pathway and through the archway, only to stop right inside it.

Everyone watches us. Simone, who must've exited the house from the side door to get out here, Isaac and the children all sitting in chairs, along with Joy — who moved into her own place a week after my arrival — while Owen stands at the end of the walkway waiting for me to come to him.

Then, when Maksim nods toward my right, my shifting gaze is met by the sight of my mother standing off to the side, softly weeping into her hands as she stares at me.

Disbelief, hope, and pure shock keep me locked where I stand as I stare at the one person I thought I would never see again. "Mama?"

Who moves first, I don't remember, but my determination not to mess my makeup is ruined when my Mama hugs me crying with the same relief and joy as me.

"How?" I ask her when she finally pulls back, handing me a handkerchief while dabbing at her eyes with one as well.

"I have made sure to start asking many questions, but in this, no questions. Men, Maksim's men, they come to me and they say you are here in America, alive, and I must leave my life there if I wish to see you again. Of course, you are my baby and there is no life for me at home without you, so I said yes and they brought me over here to you."

It's hard to believe this and when I glance back at Maksim, he merely nods and smiles, like he didn't do anything big at all. "You're...you're here to stay?"

"Yes, darling." She nods at Owen, who stands there patiently waiting along with everyone else, and her next words make me love him even more. "Now, you must go marry this wonderful man who has agreed to let me live with both of you."

"Of course, he has. A *babushka* is not a woman to mess with."

"Katya is as beautiful as you," she says after laughing, pulling me into another hug before letting go and wiping at my face, and then steps back with a cheerful smile. "Go, we will have plenty of time to speak later."

She walks toward everyone else, taking a seat near the children, and Maksim blushes when I kiss his cheek upon returning to his side. "You are a wonderful man. I will never be able to repay you."

"Just be happy, *malyshka*, that's all I ask."

"I will."

Moments later, when the man I'm going to raise children with and spend the rest of my life loving takes my hands in his, my statement becomes a promise written all over my face, and reflected in his gaze when he kisses me as his wife for the first time.

∾

Owen

My wife waits for me in bed, smiling at the day while begging for the pleasure I promised her this morning with her eyes, as I enter the room after putting Katya to bed for the night.

Some nights she wants her mama, but others, she crawls into my lap and begs me to read her a story. Like tonight, and many other nights before, with many more to come in the future. I don't want to wait another moment to make our family bigger, to have more children to love and teach and protect, which mean after undressing, I climb into bed and cover Ramona's naked form with my own.

Holding her hands captive above her head, I gaze down at her with need, knowing she'll understand as I whisper, "Ready?"

Eyes glinting, she licks her lips and seeks pleasure with a lift her hips toward mine as she wraps her legs around my waist and whispers back, "Yes, sir. More than."

Brushing my lips against her mouth, I claim her with a hard, deep thrust, groaning when her always ready for me pussy clenches around me with a delighted moan of her own.

And before either of us move, before I give us both what we want and need, I say to her the same thing I do every chance I get so she never has to wonder where she stands with me ever again. "I love you."

"I love you too, O," she responds with a pleased and contented laugh, wrapping her arms around my neck when I release them. "Now, fuck me like you mean it, sir."

She doesn't have to ask twice, and with a grin,

I show her exactly how much I mean it, now and forever.

THE END!

**Thanks so much for reading! I hope you loved reading Owen and Ramona's story.

If you enjoyed it, please consider telling your friends or posting a short review on the site you purchased this book from. Word of mouth is an author's best friend and much appreciated!**

To continue on with Joy's story, pick up a copy of **Forever Mine** today!

ABOUT THE AUTHOR

Violet Haze is a big fan of romance — writing & reading. The autistic mother of one, she currently spends her days writing, reading, procrastinating, & listening to her son play video games she doesn't understand, at all.

For information on other books you can read, including links to ALL the vendors, visit her website: www.authorviolethaze.com!

Want to contact Violet?
Email her at: violet@authorviolethaze.com or locate her at one of the links listed below!

www.ingramcontent.com/pod-product-compliance
Lightning Source LLC
Chambersburg PA
CBHW031035120726
47905CB00007B/2190